Other 1632 Universe Publications

1632 by Eric Flint created this universe. Free download available at Baen
.com/1632.html. All listed books available at Baen.com.

Short-List of Titles to Jump into the Series:

Ring of Fire anthology edited by Eric Flint

1633 by Eric Flint and David Weber

1634: The Baltic War by Eric Flint and David Weber

All books available through Baen.com, booksellers, and used book-
stores.

Also Available:

Grantville Gazette Volumes 1 – 102, magazine edited by Eric Flint, Paula
Goodlett, Walt Boyes, Bjorn Hasseler. Available on 1632Magazine.com.

1632 Universe novels and "Eric Flint, Ring of Fire Series" on Baen.com

Recently Released and Forthcoming:

Mrs. Flannery's Flowers Bethanne Kim

Gourmets of Grantville Bethanne Kim

Red Shield Bethanne Kim

Odd numbered months: New issues of Eric Flint's 1632 & Beyond

Reading Order:

There are three different reading orders available. The first is chronolog-
ical. The second is by storyline. The third is by publication date.

https://author.1632magazine.com/canon-continuity/reading-order-s
mall-bites/

Issue #15 January 2026

ERIC FLINT'S

1632
&BEYOND

Edith Wild

Bethanne Kim

Chuck Thompson

Robert F. Lowell

Marc Tyrrell

David Hankins

Jackie Britton Lopatin

ERIC FLINT'S 1632 & BEYOND ISSUE #15

This is a work of fiction. Names, characters places, and events portrayed in this book are fictional or used fictitiously. Any resemblance to real people (living or dead), or events is coincidental.

Editor-in-Chief Bjorn Hasseler
Publisher Bethanne Kim
Editor Chuck Thompson
Cover Artwork by Cortney Skinner
Interior Art Garrett W. Vance

1. Science Fiction-Alternate History
2. Science Fiction-Time Travel

eBook ISBN: 978-1-962398-33-6
Paperback ISBN: 978-1-962398-34-3

Distributed by Flint's Shards Inc.
339 Heyward Street, #200
Columbia, SC 29201

Contents

Eric Flint's *1632* & Beyond

Issue 15

As the January issue comes right before Valentine's Day, we decided to have a romance theme. The intention was that the stories would be love stories.

Our authors went in a different direction....

First, they asked if that included St. Valentine's Day massacres—and were able to cite multiple events. But in the end, they didn't go there, either.

The Merriam-Webster Dictionary has another definition of romance:

"prose narrative treating imaginary characters involved in events remote in time or place and usually heroic, adventurous, or mysterious"

(, definition 2 a (2))

We don't know whether our authors looked this up, but it's what they wrote. A couple of the stories in this issue fit definition 1, but all of them fit definition 2.

Magdeburg Messenger

(Fiction)

This issue's cover is taken from Edith Wild's story "When Jimmy Met Barbie." You met Jimmy and Barbie in her story "Come Dig My Earth" in Issue 10. This is their prequel.

"Something Old" follows up on one thread in Bethanne Kim's novel *Red Shield*, which will be released January 6. It's up to you, but you might want to save this story and read the novel first.

The Ring of Fire didn't shock just the up-timers and down-timers. It also affected their pets. Chuck Thompson focuses on one of them in "Dagnabit Belle."

In his first 1632 story, Robert F. Lowell relates "The Grand Adventure of Baron von Münchhausen in the Land of the Americans." It's about a historical down-timer who is the ancestor of the man with whom you are probably more familiar.

In Issue 12, you met Alphons and Rose in Marc Tyrrell's story "To Kill A Redbird." This issue's story "Adieu Anvers" takes place earlier.

David Hankins follows up "The Abrabanel Rescue" from Issue 14 with "The Brezelgeist Romance."

The State Library Papers
(1632 Non-Fiction)

We have three short non-fiction columns in this issue.

The first is Jackie Britton Loptain's "Mannington Minute."

"Historic Gems Restorations" is about a non-profit restoring buildings in Mannington.

The last is about next year's convention.

The Coming Soon and Available Now sections are growing again as Baen rereleases more books.

Patreon Supporters

1632 & Beyond thanks the following Patreon members who have generously agreed to help underwrite the magazine's operations.

Thank you so much for supporting us.

Gary
Pascal Durand
Marc Foppen
Sally Hardwick
Karjala Koponen
Jerry Johnson
Marc Tyrrell
David Smith
Edh Stanley
Campbell Menzies
Thomas Williams
Virginia DeMarce
Jay Robison
Chuck Thompson
Philip Stewart
Peter Jaeger
Stephanie Walton
Scott Weaver

Magdeburg Messenger
Fiction

When Jimmy Met Barbie
Edith Wild

Downtown Grantville

February 6, 1636, Wednesday

Jimmy rode his Harley up to Market on East Main just as the traffic light flicked from yellow to red. He cursed and braked, steadying the bike out of a skid into a stop, thankfully not entirely in the crosswalk. He glared down at the road, scraped to ice but not pavement, then up at the traffic light, tapping his boots. Jimmy glanced down-street at the lights flashing on the train-track gates. The evening train was growling into town like a wolf. *Damn the timing*, he thought as the cold wind chewed through his jacket like it wasn't there.

There hadn't been a sunset earlier, just the orangish dimming of the snow-laden clouds covering the winter sky to the west and north. The new moon meant the only light came from street lights and store fronts. People crowded Market Street, rushing like skittish deer towards the train station lights. He thought, *there's no way through for a while.*

Southeast of his position, the train clanged toward the station. The engineer would signal to run up on the siding, west of Mary Ellen Street.

The traffic light flicked to green. Jimmy turned the Harley 'roundabout and drove off down East Main, back-tracking.

He breathed, letting out a stream of glittering fog. Lunch was a memory—it'd been split pea and ham soup with a good chunk of rye bread and butter to sop it up. *Hot coffee,* he thought, *that would've been nice, should have grabbed it at Miller's. I should've eaten more.* Jimmy considered his options for food. There was nothing at home he wanted.

As he drove past DiCamillo's, the perfume of fresh-made pies pulled at him. He licked his lips, wanting the taste of a sour cherry pie in *that* flaky buttery crust, crusted with sugar crystals. Jimmy's sigh whitened the cold air. *I'll have to wait until the next time I'm in Prague visiting Mom. Not anytime soon.* His stomach grumbled again, scolding him for neglect. He wanted a beer. A *good* one. Maybe more than one. He deserved it. It was his birthday after all.

Deciding where to go for dinner was like ice-fishing this time of year: a lotta ponds, but iced over, no fish holes to drop a line in. The Thuringen Gardens didn't appeal. He'd been there at least a dozen times since the New Year's Eve party and was sick of it, especially the tacos. The nearest interesting place was The Hole in the Wall. At least it had novelty, as he hadn't been there since summer.

Jimmy pulled in, ice crunching under his wheels. The Hole in the Wall's street-side lot showed him he wasn't the only biker. He fit right in the row. He dismounted, fastened his helmet to his bike, and chained his Harley up. His dang bike had gone "borrowed" too many times. It'd been to Rudolstadt without him, to Saale without him, and several times to the stockyards down south without him, but the bike chain stopped the "borrowing". He still didn't know who had the extra keys to the bike.

Jimmy hoped whoever took the bike hadn't done anything stupid while he had it. A singular purple Harley was kinda obvious.

Jimmy shoved through the Hole in the Wall's doors. He hadn't known what to expect, it'd been a while. There were squawks coming from the "parrot habitat". The air was hazy with tobacco smoke, *a useless habit*. The vague burnt mix of several flavored tobaccos wafted about. He didn't gag. The aroma of food dominated everything, the scent of bay candles underlying it all.

Jimmy stuffed his gloves and wool hat into the pockets of his leather coat and hung it on the crowded coat tree next to the door. He ran his hands through his hair to smooth it. His Sharps-Hankins pepperbox pistol was on his hip, brass knuckles in his pocket. Wanted posters tacked up by the front door included a bad photo of a large dog. He snorted.

Over the bar was a brand-new sign calligraphed in gold and white: *Cap'n Gars Bar, est. 1633.* Jimmy moved through a group of bikers leaving the bar, and realized he knew the barkeep. "Rothrock! Are you slumming? Aren't you a paramedic?" Amused, he slid onto a stool at the long wood bar.

Rothrock laughed, eyes crinkling. "Hell, not always. I work here some-times." He made a coin-rubbing motion with his fingers. "What do you want?"

Jimmy chuckled. "Beer at least. Do you have any Augustiner Bräu München?" He rested his elbows on the counter and leaned in. "And dinner. What's on the menu that's decent? You pick."

Rothrock nodded. "We have that on tap." He poured Jimmy the Au-gustiner while he talked, keeping three conversations going at once. Jimmy sipped the beer as Rothrock turned, saying something brief to a nearby serving woman. Nodding, she went through the kitchen's swinging door, the smell of cooking food wafting out before it swung shut.

Jimmy relaxed, finally. He'd been busy all day. His stack of invoices at the counter in Miller's was the easy bit. The office was a waste of patience if *she* was there. At some point between deliveries, he'd heard a banging start up inside the warehouse and stomped back through the office and warehouse, ignoring *Marlene* and *her glare,* shutting the dang door. *Marlene* wasn't there on his way back. Midafternoon, he had to go back to his first delivery in Rudolstadt. *Someone* had screwed up the morning order. Mrs. Kinney's fault. She was *all over*—not just at the register—putting blame wherever. He'd been late on a couple deliveries because of Rudolstadt when it was *her* screw up. But he took it. At least the truck's heater worked. And it had gotten him away from her!

Jimmy swore softly and drank more beer, then set the glass down carefully on the bar. He turned on the bar stool, looking over the pool tables. Among his considerations was whether he should stay any length of time. Jimmy observed a good dozen people following a lively match, chattering away. Bets were obviously on *that* match. Several were up-time bikers he knew slightly, all togged up in leathers.

Beyond the pool tables was the dining room. Indistinct conversations overlapped and muddled, punctuated by clacking balls on the blue felt of the white-painted pool tables.

Jimmy turned back and grabbed his beer. Rothrock had moved along, serving someone else. Jimmy didn't mind losing his attention. Thursday nights weren't overly busy. Service was good. The bar felt better, so he stayed there. Up-time music spun in the background.

The server slipped a large plate and a bowl in front of Jimmy. The plate held hot cabbage rolls stuffed with chopped roasted pork and sauced with a tomato glaze, butter noodles, and the ubiquitous sauerkraut. It smelled wonderful, and it was *hot*. In the bowl was a beautiful roasted apple sweetened with a touch of honey. He ate that first. Delicious.

Jimmy had no intentions other than filling his belly, downing a few beers, and going to his little house. He'd finished supper, got wrapped up in watching a couple of pool matches. Butcher, one of the bikers he knew, looked over and called, "Hey, Wildman!"

Jimmy heard himself asking, "Ya wanna set?"

Butcher laughed, "I'm pretty bored. Not that you could beat me!"

So they played like the two lost souls from the old Club 250 that they were. It was lively.

Their talk had them laughing at bad jokes spiked with rambling tall tales, but turning serious on engines, spare parts, and availability. And, of course, women. Underneath their conversation was the clacking of pool cues and the sound of the balls hitting and dancing across the table. Jimmy won a few coins and a free beer with a large soft pretzel served with good mustard. And the cheeses! It was nice since he was thirsty again and somewhat hungry. Some of the original crowd had left and been replaced with new folks. He wasn't sure how long he'd been there. Two hours, maybe three?

He glanced up at a herd of nurses from Leahy Medical strolling in through the double wood doors, laughing and chatting, biting cold air blowing in with them. They must have walked over from the hospital. *Whatever floats 'em*, Jimmy thought. One of the nurses yelled to Rothrock in German, "Beers, beers, beers for us all and a table for twelve just in case!"

The parrots in the parrot room squealed and chanted.

One of the nurses wore a dark red cloak, hood dropped down her back. The cloak looked warm, wooly, and well cared for. She tossed her crazy-curly, barely tied-up hair back over her shoulder. When she talked to another woman, he saw her teeth were all there, not always the case with down-timers. *Up-timer? Down-timer?* Jimmy sighed. Down-time women tended to be much shorter than up-time women, but not always. Not petite, not plump. Jimmy decided he liked her face, so he watched and drank his beer.

After a little while she reached up to push back the mass of curls again with her left hand; her ringer and pinks looked oddly scarred. *That's old,* he thought, *how the hell didn't she lose those fingers?* Jimmy watched more intently, feeling curious. She was *interesting*.

He asked Rothrock when he got close to Jimmy's end of the bar, "What's with that nurse? The one with the hand?"

"Oh," Rothrock said, "Her?" He nodded in the right direction.

The old CD mixer started playing a lost up-time band's song, *"Stuck in a Moment You Can't Get Out Of."*

"Yes, her."

Rothrock glanced towards the nurses, then looked at Jimmy. "That's Barbara Schmidt. Barbie. She's a nurse."

Jimmy, raising an eyebrow at *"Barbie"*, drank some more beer. "What's with her hand?"

Rothrock glared at Jimmy. "Is it important? You focus on that?"

He shook his head, "No, no. It looks like a really vicious dueling scar. Like someone almost took her fingers off. But women don't duel." Jimmy ran his fingers back and forth through a ring of condensation on the dark wood bar top.

"Women do not duel," Rothrock agreed. "But they can...fight. The scar...well, it does not impede."

"So she can use her hand?" Jimmy prompted.

"Of course," said Rothrock.

Something about her was interesting. And Rothrock was being weird about her, which made her more interesting. "Who did she fight?"

"Why should I tell you?" Rothrock's face twitched a bit. Jimmy wondered what he was trying to hide. Or if he was being too annoying. Jimmy was good at being annoying.

He shrugged and lifted his glass, but his glass was empty. He frowned. He thought it was the fourth one.

He looked over towards the other end of the bar. The herd of nurses must have vanished into the back somewhere. He had been back there last summer for a picnic. The Hole in the Wall was a series of odd rooms cobbled together, several big enough to actually make a nice-sized dining room. There was a separate bar with a lunch counter, big enough for a take out and delivery system. Way out back, *Cap'n Gars Grill, est. 1634,* was a barbeque for ribs or roasts or whatever, normally going in all sorts of weather.

The song *"Stuck in a Moment You Can't Get Out Of"* finished. Jimmy said to Rothrock, "More beer. Who's spinning the music?"

"The Jenss boys, Anton and Ludwig, over there."

"Ah, I see." He saw a pair of harlequin coats in gold and green and fancy hair.

As Rothrock was pouring Jimmy another Augustiner, he asked off-handedly, quietly, "Do you want to meet her?"

"I dunno," Jimmy said, feeling uneasy. *That gal can fight?* He was missing something.

The next song, *"House of the Rising Sun,"* began while Jimmy drank his beer and nibbled on another soft pretzel, dipping it in mustard. At some point he heard a cheerful feminine voice say in lightly accented English, "Hey, Rothrock! We need more beer!"

Jimmy side-eyed her, watching, listening. Her voice was nice. He liked listening to *that* voice. Close-up, the dark red cloak looked even prettier on her. He remembered her name, Barbie. She looked tired. Her eyes were grayish, large and lively. She was not a redhead, not dark-haired either. Her curly hair was the sort of amber brown that streaks blondish in the summer sun.

Then she noticed him, glared, and rolled her eyes as she looked away.

Jimmy felt the flush crawl up his face.

"Got it, Barbie. You all want a pitcher, right?" Rothrock asked.

Ignoring Jimmy completely, she said, "Large, please! Danke! We'll need two. Oh, and we want the Maine grill. Okay? Make sure that battered cod is really crispy. Oh, Doro wants to have that carp with it!" Barbie then asked, "Hey, can you light my cigar?" She lifted it in her left hand, the scar plainly visible. She side-eyed Jimmy for sure.

"Got it." Rothrock leaned in closely, lit her cigar. "The cod's been salted, dried, and hydrated, rinsed, then battered and fried."

"That's fine." Barbie looked back at Jimmy and glared at him as she wandered off to the back dining room. Smoking. Jimmy noted the length of her curly hair, practically to her waist, loosely tied. That meant something...but the meaning escaped him.

Rothrock disappeared through the swinging door into the kitchen.

The song had changed again to *"Summer of Love."* Not obnoxious.

"Cigar? Maine grill?" Jimmy asked Rothrock when he got back from the kitchen.

Rothrock cleared his throat. "Yep. Smoking is a thing, we offer it, so do some of the other restaurants. It's been here for a while, not cheap, not particularly ordinary, smells. Hate it, really. You don't approve?"

Jimmy shrugged. "It's stupid." He sounded nastier than he'd meant to. "So. Maine grill?"

Rothrock raised an eyebrow. "Okay. Alright. So. We do several kinds of fish, locally fished, farmed, or brined or smoked and dried. We get some fish imports from Cuxhaven in Saxony. There's fries and onion rings, as I understand it, oh, and coleslaw, not sauerkraut."

Jimmy grinned, teasing, "Saxony? All that way? That port? There's a way? I've been there, a while back, up-time. So. You're selling food now? Not spelunking idiots off into jail? Not mending the broken?"

Rothrock laughed, tapped his hand on the bar. "It's winter. Too cold for spelunking the fools. Someone's gotta feed the parrots and pour the beers. Gotta pay the bills, Wildman, between ambulance runs!"

Jimmy laughed, sipped his beer, and appreciated it. Glared over at the noisy parrot room at the very end of the long bar. The birds had come with Grantville. Those damn birds were squawking again and cursing at each other. The parrot room had several active breeding pairs, and stank like a dovecote when the doors weren't shut.

Rothrock went back into the kitchen, muttering about needing to restock something. Jimmy drank some more beer. Wondering if he should ask for water next time.

The music playing in the background was some Kidz Bop version of "Macarena." He wrinkled his nose. If it was a joke, it wasn't fun for his ears. He wondered who it was for, what it meant, if anything.

The birds started to settle, then someone walked in front of the parrot room on the way to the water-toilet and the damn birds started up, screaming curses in German and English and what sounded like pig Latin. The birds continued to scream at another man who hadn't left his cloak on the coat tree.

Jimmy stared at the guy with the cloak. He caught a whiff of bloodiness as the man went past him. The man was none too clean in other respects, like he'd been sweating all day and running with dogs in the damn cold weather. *He's armed,* Jimmy thought, *he stinks of gunpowder and blood.* Jimmy fingered his holstered gun for a moment, staring at the cloaked man.

That man was heading to where that dame, that Barbie girl, went back toward the Cap'n Gars Grill to be outside with the rest of the herd of nurses.

Jimmy considered if he might do anything. Shrugged, drank down his beer. As he was setting down the mug, someone started yelling from the back. The song in the background switched into "I Can't Get No Satisfaction." At first, he thought it was the parrots shrieking. But it wasn't.

Someone threw the back doors open letting in a rush of cold air. A man's voice bellowed loud enough to be heard over the music, several others were nearly as loud. "Get it away! Get it away! It's a monster!"

A man's voice cracked loudly as a scream rang out, "Throw it!"

In a few seconds Jimmy got it. The screaming was terrifying, like a banshee in panic. The memory almost came on then, almost a jeep flipping. Jimmy dumped the barstool with a crash, running towards the fracas. Felt sober for a minute. The bouncer streamed right by him, then Rothrock, Butcher, and a couple of the biker dudes from the pool tables. Some people pushed their way past him to the main room, getting away, panic on their faces. Jimmy followed the screams. Rothrock and the bouncer led the way, running to and shoving through the back door.

There was growling, then loud howls from out back.

The fire pit was lit, bright in the dark. The herd of nurses had been enjoying it and their beers here instead of inside the dining room. The weird guy with the cloak wasn't visible. There was considerable noise in the bushes behind the firepit and barbeque. And growling.

Then *it* emerged. Headed to the barbeque where ribs and steaks were grilling. *It* was a very large, huge, dog. Sharp-toothed, snarling, fair colored, thickly furred, eyes like hot coals. In that flickering light from the fire pit it almost looked like a German shepherd, only much, much bigger. Gigantic.

It took a long moment, then Jimmy recognized what it was. It had to be sick. He tried to remember what a wolf could be sick with.

"Wolf! There's a goddamn wolf here!" Jimmy yelled, his voice slurred. He felt dizzy. Dammit, he drank too much. He picked up a fist-sized stone from a small pile and threw it. He missed, just made the wolf angrier. Someone else threw another rock, landing it closer to the wolf. It moved quickly, growling louder.

Jimmy pulled his Sharps and Hankins pepperbox gun, shot at the wolf, reloaded.

The wolf ran, leaving crimson drips. Howling. The huntsman in the smelly cloak ran by him, after the wolf. Jimmy almost felt sympathy for the wolf.

The nurses had vanished like deer. *Back inside, maybe?* Jimmy hoped that the Barbie-nurse was with them. Maybe it didn't matter. It didn't matter. Jimmy yelled, "The chase is on," running down the 250 towards Leahy, screaming, "He-yaa!"

As he ran after both the wolf and the cloaked dude, Jimmy heard the big bad wolf song in his head and thought, *Dammit! Fairy tales!*

February 7, 1636, Thursday

No Harley today. Jimmy's head danced in the hangover. His Harley's gas tank was low, but that'd wait until payday. Jimmy walked from the bus stop to Miller's Hardware Store on Rose. A kid in a red cap was hawking newspapers, so he bought one, dropping a quarter in the cup. His major worries for today were pretty crushed: somebody was subbing for him today. So, Jimmy slept in—*after* Mr. Miller called him, told him to take the morning, come in later.

It took less than ten minutes, bus stop to work, walking in the snarling cold.

He was fixed into the hardware store, stuck there for years, snow, sleet, winter, summer. Once inside what he thought of as *his* building, Miller's Hardware, he went from freezing to almost warm. There was the added heat of a wood-burning pot belly stove in the middle of things, on top of a slab of concrete, where it had been since January of 1632. There was talk of replacing it with a *kakelugn,* that Swedish stove.

On the front counter between the cash registers was a crockpot full of stew meat in gravy, smelling like venison. A side plate had roasted potatoes and other root veggies. There was good bread and butter. Someone had got a box of shortbread cookies from DiCamillo's, the thumbprint filling dark pink. Someone else had brought a tiny plate of what looked like chocolate chip cookies, so expensive. Everything looked wonderful, smelled great. Everyone was waiting on him, talking. Butcher was leaning against the counter, laughing at a joke.

"What's all this for?" Jimmy blinked in confusion.

His boss laughed and clapped his shoulder. "You saved the nurses! Didn't you read your headline?"

"Uh, not yet," Jimmy said, feeling uncomfortable. "They took pictures of me and that huntsman guy from Rudolstadt. I wasn't expecting anything. Really."

"You made the HEADLINE! Good job! Good publicity! Let's eat!"

Jimmy nodded, carefully unfolding the newspaper. The photograph's caption under the headline read, *"Local man helps Rudolph Jaegerson of Rudolstadt capture and kill a record-size dangerous wolf...it was measured at 35 inches on the withers, over six feet long, and weighed 215 pounds. There were three other wolves taken prior...The men will split the bounty.*

"The high school's Science Department chair, Herr Tony Mastroianni, explained, 'Basically, this is just a big wolf, not a dire wolf, as those have been extinct for ten thousand years. Most likely just a very large and well-fed grey wolf subspecies.' Several local farmers relayed to us that there were many more of these huge wolves; this was the fourth killed in the last few weeks. One farmer, Gunter Schafmann, said he'd lost eight sheep since last November to wolves, tracked, with signs of giant paws. As to why it went to the barbeque area, crowded with people, management believes it was the fresh meat."

Jimmy hated the killing of the wolf, its eyes mournful as it stared at the huntsman. Jimmy understood from the huntsman that this was not the only huge wolf that the man had hunted. There was a big pack of them, all tremendous in size. *Ice-Age predators? Here?*

Jimmy grimaced as he finished the article. Sure, it was sheer dumb luck on his part, but his bank account was going to be happier. *Dire wolves? Can't be.*

Quitting Time, Miller's Hardware Store Off Rose Street February 21, 1636

Marlene screamed at him finally. She'd been running hot every time he came in. He took it. She made it plenty loud and long so everyone could hear. "Your bookkeeping stinks! You got this receipt made out to the wrong party and the wrong amount! Is that a 140 or a 190? You can't add, asshole!"

"I, what?"

"You heard me. The till is short! You stupid thieving monster!"

He shouted, "I don't steal!"

Her voice grated, "Ha! What's in your pocket? You're a lying headcase!"

"I don't freaking steal!"

"You evil bastard!" Marlene threw an old-fashioned inkwell at him. It missed but shattered, bleeding black ink on the floor.

Jimmy shut up. He stomped outta Miller's, boots loud. Slammed that glass door behind him. He heard the crack. It startled him, then he took a step without looking down, skidded.

A gaggle of kids dashed in front of him dropping coins and stuff, shiny. Jimmy tried to avoid them and a much older man having trouble walking the patchy wet and iced sidewalk. Jimmy tried to stop moving. The sidewalk was frictionless under his cowboy boots. He'd hand-salted and sanded the ice twice already since lunch and scraped it up each time after. Yet it was like someone spilt water on the pavement.

The cold snatched Jimmy's breath away, leaving him gasping. The constant wind made everything unbearable. It'd been 17°F out his sitting room window only this morning, but this freeze-down surprised him. The thermometer at Miller's said -2°F, so it was colder. The weather had been especially sloppy-cold, melting and refreezing before Valentine's Day and his wolf encounter. Jimmy slid, twirled, lost his balance, and wobbled, trying to regain it. He felt his right knee cracking back, moving *wrong*, and then he fell. The sidewalk was unforgiving.

He lay there, just breathing. The ice was cold on his ass and back. And wet. *Black ice. I'm so stupid. It's wet?*

Jimmy hadn't hit his head. That was the only positive. He winced. *I hit my funny bone.* His fingers tingled. He wiggled them, first his left hand, looked at it carefully, then his right, same. No excessive pain there. Jimmy shut his eyes. Tried not to curse. Failed. At least he wasn't too loud. All his words left his brain.

He didn't even try to move anything else. This was bad. His leg was bad. His hip, nearly. Fear was a monster. Jimmy tried to keep breathing calmly. It was hard. His leg *hurt*. Pain radiated like fire.

Those kids and the old man were gone. It didn't sound like anyone else was around. Randomly, he noticed silver coins on the black ice.

A tear leaked out of his right eye. He shut his eyes. He was dizzy, and memories ran out of hiding. The Somalia mission from 1993 threatened, flooding back, as a landmine, a humvee, loomed in his mind. The humvee in the very front had not survived. He'd survived. His humvee wasn't in the front. Jimmy shoved those thoughts away. He lay there alone, stunned, breathing hard. If he opened his mouth, he'd start screaming. That wasn't safe.

There were footsteps, voices. A vaguely familiar woman's voice whispered in German something he didn't catch. Then the voice said in English, "Shut it up, Mrs. Kinney. I am tending to him until the ambulance gets here."

"How dare you! You, you!"

The voice came on aggravated, not patient, "I am a nurse, I am medically trained." She whispered something to Jimmy he could not quite hear.

Daphne's voice said, "Mother!"

"Don't take that side, Daphne! Go away! Why should he get medical help for being drunk! What do you expect from, from, from a drunkard murdering bastard?" Mrs. Kinney shouted, "That man is a bad one! They should have hanged him when they had a chance! My Geri would be—"

"Now, mother, this is public!" Daphne warned.

Mrs. Kinney yelled, "You are as bad as he is!" There was the sound of a blistering smack on bare skin.

"Mother!" Daphne gasped. Outraged boot stomping went back into the hardware store. Another set of footsteps followed.

Jimmy moaned.

The other voice said to Jimmy in German, "Shush. She's a moonsick rat."

Jimmy hadn't been drunk since the run-in with the wolf. He could've hurt someone, if his aim had been worse. *I'm not perfect. Hell, no one is.* At least, he wasn't a monster. Not that Mrs. Kinney cared. She always believed the worst of him for a lot of reasons.

The door opened again. Didn't shut. There was crying inside.

Ken Miller, his boss, said fiercely, "Marlene! He is not drunk or loaded on anything. He had nothing to do with Geri being murdered in Jena! Now is not the time to rake that old damned tragedy over the coals and make it burn your soul again."

Mrs. Kinney snorted. "Jena! Such a smart choice! University town!"

More footsteps. Mr. Miller asked, "Waldo! You called for the ambulance?"

"Ja. Five minutes, boss! Nurse Schmidt asked me to. She was here to pick up more of those trays."

Mrs. Kinney found her voice, yelled, "Why not? Why not make him burn again? He deserved this!" Her tone had so much hate in it. "He made Geri into a whore! His choices killed her!"

Jimmy lay there for that eternity stunned, eyes closed. Trying to breathe through the pain. The thought surfaced, *She still hates me? I didn't kill Geri. I never hurt her in any way. I am innocent of that.* The creeping horror was nauseating. It had little to do with his leg. He knew why the sidewalk was wet. He knew what the coin meant. He shivered. The one minute he was off his watch!

"Marlene! No. He did not," Mr. Miller sounded worried, angry, "What did you do?"

"Ha! Like I'd say!" Mrs. Kinney said. Her voice sounded weird, like she was hiding something badly.

Jimmy shivered then. It wasn't from the cold.

The sirens were closing in. He heard something large and mechanical stop. Heard doors groan open. Heard distantly voices shouting instructions, in German of one sort and English of another. Knew one voice for certain. Heard some loud clicking. Cracked his eyes open to Rothrock and others rolling a gurney over, closed his eyes. Heard Rothrock's voice close by say, "We gotta immobilize..."

In a moment or so, he felt the slide of the backboard under him, momentary agony, his limbs carefully arranged, then the lift onto the gurney and the lift of the gurney.

Jimmy fainted, thinking, *I hope they keep that lunatic away from me!*

Leahy Medical
February 22, 1636

Jimmy blinked. Realization set in. The space smelled of antiseptic, not heaven as he might have wished for. Leahy Medical was the only answer to a question he could not ask anyone just yet.

It hadn't been a PTSD dream, he was certain, it didn't stop the misery of long-set heartache. The dream had seemed real. A moment ago, he'd been dreaming of long dead and buried Geri. She'd been repeating her last fiercest argument with him for *that day*, but nothing he'd said had changed her replies. He'd been holding her for God's sake. He could still feel the warmth and weight of her body against his. He could almost smell her perfume, her voice whispering, *"You didn't kill me."*

He almost felt her hand touch his face.

"I left you alone," Jimmy whispered to himself. He shook his head, concentrating on breathing. His mouth tasted like old dry cotton. His tongue was dry. His throat was dry. He wanted water. None in sight.

The echo of her voice said, *"No."*

He was stuck on his back like a turtle. Counted down from three and tried to roll over. It hurt. More than a bit, not just his leg. Jimmy exhaled. He looked over at the pole he was hooked to. A glass saline flask with the not very flexible tubing hung there. Wondered what meds he was on. There was one in particular he was *not* supposed to use, *Don't want to get rehooked*. Reconsidered trying to move again.

He was alone in a proper hospital room. The windowpane shadows flickered across the whitewashed walls. His door wasn't closed. He ignored the sound of the voices, the swift footsteps that came down the hallway. It wasn't his business to know that stuff, *It's intruding*.

Jimmy tried to adjust himself for comfort's sake. His position on the hospital bed was understandable. His moves to fix the pain were just wrong. Jimmy lay there, gasping, for a quick minute staring at that white ceiling, at the damn acoustic tiles. A tear trickled out of his right eye, unbidden. His whole right leg hurt from hip to ankle, like the pain meds he shouldn't have had were fading. His toes were cold, numbed. *I wish I had socks!*

He was in a genuine hospital bed, left from before the Ring of Fire, slightly sloped to elevate his head. Jimmy strained to look at his leg as best he might. His right foot stuck out in an old up-time immobilizer, velcroed tight. It was an artifact if it had velcro. It also appeared clean and dark blue, if faded. He could tell that much. The rest of him was under covers, relatively warm.

He spotted the worn buzzer clamped onto the bed and pushed it.

Jimmy noticed the calves of his well-worn cowboy boots under the console across the room from him. Next to that table was a coat rack, his winter coat hanging on it. His street clothes were on a hanger. On top of the console were his antiquated brass knuckles, wallet, keys, his small penknife in ivory with silver trim of WW I vintage, grandpa's, even the hunting knife. The gun wasn't there. Directly next to the window was a big padded chair, vaguely familiar. Jimmy blinked.

In less than a minute Doc Adams showed up with two orderlies, telling them to take care of him. The orderlies, both men, unhooked him from the saline bottle and all sorts of things he had no names for. They helped him to the toilet. Then, back. But not to the hospital bed. They took him to that big chair in the corner by the window. The chair seemed big enough for three people.

One of the orderlies said, "It's one of the power-lift chairs, don't be afraid."

"This is weird. A power-lift chair?" Jimmy's thoughts moved quickly. *It's grainy blue, oh, Jeez, it's not* that *one, is it?* "Oh. Oh. Those chairs were a thing." Jimmy gritted against the pain of a different kind. *My dad used one, when he was dying from black lung.* He ran a finger under the edge of the chair's right arm. He found the hole in the metal, where the drip had been clipped. *Oh, gawd*, he thought, *I did that?*

As both orderlies helped him arrange and elevate his leg, one of them called the other Rudy. The pain in his knee stopped for a minute.

Doc Adams strolled back in, all casual. He said, "Hey, Dennis, Rudy, give us the room." The orderlies left. He asked, "Do you want the good news or the bad news first, Jimmy?"

Jimmy whispered, "You know what I need. Bad news first, doc."

Doc Adams, who did not sit but stood, explained, "Okay. You suffered a break of your right tibial plateau, your knee." Then he said, "Your right hip is bruised, not broken."

Jimmy cursed a lot. He knew exactly what that injury was.

Doc Adams waited. He said, "We were able to fix it well enough. However, you won't be able to ride your Harley for about twelve weeks. Or drive, as it is your right knee. You're just temporarily damaged."

Jimmy heard himself spit out another curse word. "So what's the good news, Doc, besides I won't lose my leg or die? That my hip is only bruised? I'm on damned repeat. Seems like."

Doc Adams waited, "You're right, your leg will be better than it was last time. This was successful. So, a *Schatzker IV.* Your tibial plateau fractured into a bunch of pieces. A football injury essentially. I drained your break. Your bone fragments went back in with a little persuasion. We pinned. Your meniscus did not roll up or tear."

"So?" Jimmy asked.

Doc Adams spoke, "We were able to get an immobilizer on you. Jimmy, you will wear it without fail for eight weeks. We're keeping you for a week to get you started on your physical therapy. Once done with therapy, your already-present limp will have diminished."

Jimmy sighed.

Doc Adams stared at him. "Well, it's up to you. The more dedicated you are to physical therapy the better the results."

"I already have a limp. Somalia, the landmine thing that blew up that Humvee in front of us. This can only get worse."

Doc Adams jotted something on his notepad. "Ah. Alright. I'm making a note about gait-training. Your nurse, Barbie Schmidt, will assign the physical therapy. You had no other injuries from that landmine incident in 1993?" He paused. "Somalia?"

Jimmy shook his head, distracted. "I was in two places, three actually. The Gulf War and Kuwait for me were safe, Somalia was not. I wasn't in the direct line, otherwise I'd be dead or crippled or blind."

Doc Adams wrote fast. "Oh. It was bad?"

He exhaled, swallowed. "It was October of '93. We were in three hummers leading an equipment caravan." He stopped, heard it all again, then swallowed and said, "Eight casualties. All three hummers were in tailbed configuration. I was in the last, last seat, passenger side, last hummer. I was in Germany, Landstuhl, after, to recover."

Doc Adams looked at him hard. Jimmy saw it. The man changed the subject immediately, "Incidentally, Jimmy, we found an old CPM machine, a plug-in." He cleared his throat.

Jimmy said, "You found one of those here?"

Doc Adams went on. "The machine was at one of the old nursing homes in a storage closet. Apparently, whoever checked it disregarded it. The last time the CPM got used was in 1996. The team borrowed it for an injured player."

"Yep. That." Jimmy remembered. That kid's future career in football was over before it could start. Jimmy pondered, "How did you find it, the machine? You haven't said who told you."

Adams had trouble speaking, starting and stopping. He finally said, "Linda."

Jimmy was unsure of anything just then, "Damn! You talked to *her*?"

"Not directly. Ham radio. That's what she said to Nurse Schmidt. Doesn't have time to dither with your problems, whatever they are. She said to say that to you. She has babies. She's staying in Jena. Her husband was not sanguine about her even communicating the existence of the CPM." He paused, then said, "She insisted to him she had to tell someone. Linda was listed as your emergency contact."

"Wait a minute, *was*? She'd agreed!" Jimmy said. *We don't get along*, but he trusted her to not kill him if he was hurt. It was one of the few things that they did agree on after the divorce. Mostly, so that if something went really wrong, she'd know about it and be able to tell the boys.

"She is not now. Dr. Wettin insisted. He described your personality as unkind, choleric, quick to anger. He said your bile is off, you need to fix that. He still has regard for the four humors," Doc Adams said.

As his brain boiled, he felt like it folded into some origami bit to try not to rip. Jimmy yelled, "So who did he scream at?"

"Nurse Barbara Schmidt. Then called her a few choice words. She cried," Doc Adams said, voice calm. His eyes weren't.

"I thought he was supposed to be *nice*." Jimmy snapped.

"Wettin's an aristocrat. Some are only well-mannered when it is to their advantage," Doc Adams said, carefully. "Wettin called Nurse Schmidt a *hure*, among other things. Schmidt gave the phone to Nurse Dorothea Bayern."

Jimmy just sat there, stunned. "My freaking ex-wife's new husband called that nurse *that*?"

"Don't worry, Nurse Bayern dealt with it, she walked the handset over to Gary. He screamed back, in German, quite foul. Didn't take it."

"Good." Jimmy groaned. "Lambert's a tough nut. Who's my emergency contact now?"

"Up to you," Doc Adams said. He left, going down the hall to finish his rounds, the tapping of his boots fading away.

"Jeeze!" Jimmy wasn't sure why he was so angry. Or for who, for himself or for Barbie. Maybe both. He didn't bother to worry about Linda. Her choices were her own, *that toxic, self-serving, cussed shrew!* His worries for his boys made his head hurt. He was really bothered by the chair he was sitting in. *I didn't say anything about this chair!*

Jimmy Wild's House; Miller's Hardware Store on Rose Street
Friday, February 29, 1636

Ken Miller brought Joe Luthier and Ben Straub, his warehouse crew, and drove his truck up to Wild's singlewide. He parked and they piled out, staring up at the tiny building. Miller noted the adaptations to the singlewide mobile hugging the hill up along Little Mod Run. There were at least eight mobiles hanging further up the hill along a squiggly path strewn with stairs, and what used to be Downs United Methodist Church was just a driveway farther. These days, it was a synagogue. He vaguely knew at least some of those trailers had an out-of-town landlord, in Prague. *Her.* No one wanted to deal with *her. Jimmy, yes. But not his mother.*

Jimmy had done stuff. Miller stood there, hands on hips, and "hmmm-phed."

A secondary square-cut log wall was added to the outside. The roof's slope looked good, admirable. Miller thought, *It's the Little Ice Age. Wild is not an idiot. Anyone sensible does stuff to stay warm.* Joe and Ben carried the wood for the woodburning stove—the *kakelugn*—and food and drink for the fridge.

They'd stopped for a couple of minutes on the snow-drifted cement patio, looking up at the singlewide. "This really is not practical," Miller said after another minute.

Joe nodded. "Herr Miller, we broom off the patio, like the front walk at work? And sand it?"

"Yes, please."

The narrow steps up from the small cement patio went to the even smaller roofed porch and entry. The patio was street level on one side but the street sloped down on the other, which required several steps, probably should've been more where Little Mod Road sat. The narrow patio was hardly far enough back from the road. Mr. Miller said aloud, "This is too narrow here."

Ben agreed, saying, "*Ja. Ja*, Herr Miller, *sehr schmal*, uh, tight."

Joe nodded, said something back in German—Swabian or something—seemed to be in agreement.

They went up the stairs. The storm door got stuck on a screw head sticking up on the threshold. He looked; there were...numerous other screwheads. *That's new looking, Jimmy wouldn't have done that...* Miller raised his eyebrow. "I'll fix that for Jimmy. Get the tool kit from the truck."

Joe said, "*Ja*, Herr Miller!"

It was short work. The heavy wood door made of oak sealed out the cold. Someone, likely Jimmy, had turned several layers of oiled leather into weather stripping edging the outside of the wood door, nailed into the doorframe. It was filled with rope, but ruined by the screwheads that had been pounded in. Miller used the plain old key to open the lock, pushed the door inwards. Ken Miller and Joe and Ben stood there for a time at the threshold, not quite going in—not wanting to, really.

The three of them went into Jimmy Wild's shockingly tidy, sparsely furnished singlewide mobile home with the filled-in extension in front. The "front" room was larger than Miller expected, not that anything was large about the singlewide. *At least I talked him into giving me his key.* Ken Miller thought about it. This half of the divided singlewide looked like it was refurbished when Jimmy had stopped trying to live with the ex-wife, Linda, sometime in the '90s, maybe 1997? He didn't know the details, not that he wanted any of it.

"This is so not practical." He sighed. *He's coming home today.*

Miller said to Ben, who was better in English than Joe, "So. Check the pilot light for the heater, the hot water tank, um, like I've taught you. Then make sure the hot water tank is actually warm. Set the heater to..."—he looked; it was set at 55°F—"put it at 65°F. Make sure the *kakelugn* has a bit of wood in it to up the heat a bit. Wild will be home by this afternoon. Oh, and bring in the cot and things for the aide." It hadn't been lit since the morning of the accident. Then he noticed the windows. *Damn, Jimmy put up another set of glass windows over the first, inside? Wood-framed? When did that happen? Where did he get those?*

Ben said, "*Ja*, boss. Those are out there, the *hintertür*, I mean to say, back door?"

"I expect."

Ben went out. Came back inside, shrugged. "It's just a shed."

Miller sighed, took a look through several tidy closets, until, "The furnace is in here and so is the water heater."

The whole space appeared clean, not what he'd expected. Joe made quick work of putting the groceries into Jimmy's fridge and cabinets, not much but enough to get him by for a couple of days.

The men moved around, getting their tasks done. Jimmy had an easy chair and a small table with a lamp in the "front" room near the *kakelugn*. There was a bookcase filled with maybe three hundred, four hundred books, mostly science fiction, almost all hardcover. One book was left out with a paper marker in it. Miller stopped to think, *Jimmy's younger brother, Gray, collected science fiction, left it behind, obviously. Does Jimmy even realize its value? He reads?*

The shadow box with Jimmy's purple heart from the thing in Somalia in '93. An unlit candle sat next to that. A young woman's picture sat next to the candle in a pretty frame. In a moment he realized who she'd been. He whispered, "Jeeze, he's grieving over her, still?" The faded picture was of a vibrant Geri Kinney at maybe twenty years old, taken several years before the Ring of Fire, without the heavy Goth makeup she'd favored at the time. No hardness there. Marlene Kinney would blow-out if she knew. Maybe even kill Jimmy, literally. *She's already tried at least once.* Miller decided not to mention any of that even if asked. *I'm not letting that woman near here, she's brooding over the whole damned mess again.*

The *kakelugn* was now lit and warming. If Jimmy's whole side of the singlewide was even near seven hundred square feet including the winter-ized porch, Ken would be surprised. On the wall over the bookcase were family photos, including Jimmy's younger brother Grayson and his wife and family. Eleven months between the two of them. Jimmy had been born in February of '67. The sister was a year and a half younger than Grayson. Theodora—Dorrie—and her boyfriend of that moment were in another picture. The Wildman's siblings were long since out of Grantville by 1992. Ken Miller forgot which one of those had gone to Penn State to study math, working on a Ph.D., and which one was the chemical engineer eventually teaching over at Fairmont State.

There was Jimmy's *balalaika* he'd gotten in Germany when he was sta-tioned there during his recovery from that thing in Somalia at Mogadishu. Miller had heard that story from—he couldn't remember. *Balalaikas are Russian, aren't they?* Miller shook his head.

A little square turquoise 1950s dinette table strewn in silver stars with matching chairs occupied the dining area. Miller assumed the set was stolen from somewhere. Miller walked over to the short hallway, peered into Jimmy's tiny bedroom, just looking. Everything was neat. The full bed was shoved in a corner. There was a dresser and a lamp, just as barren as everything and everywhere else. The bathroom was antiseptic. He went back to the "front" room. The kitchen did in fact run along one wall. The fridge was clean and very spare, almost nothing in it even with what they'd brought. Miller thought, *This is really only a place to sleep*, but said, "This place is so lonely."

Miller looked out the window down to the freshly swept patio. Saw the storage shed at the end of the patio, muttered, "So that's where he puts his Harley." The other end held the trash can and the recycle bin.

Miller, exasperated, said, "This is not going to work. He won't be able to use the stairs properly for at least a month, maybe two. That's why he needs an aide. Hmpf." Miller wondered at the expense. Looking at the outside stair railing, it was metal. Miller wondered if wrapping that with rope would make it easier to use. "Hey, Joe, get these rails wrapped in rope, nice and tight. There's some in the back of the truck."

"*Ja*, Boss, *ich verstehe, gschwend ich werde es jetzt tun!*"

At least it sounded like that.

Once back at the hardware store, Miller needed a place to put the exercise bike and weight-lifting equipment and so on delivered from... He asked, of anyone, "Where did this stuff come from?"

Larry Dotson, the stock clerk, answered. "The Tech School, I think, or the high school's weight room. Both, maybe. Lambert signed off on it and sent it on here. There's a list of nurses who are supposed to be on some kind of rotation with Wild."

"There's a list. Here."

"Ok." Miller looked over the list Larry handed him. Some of the names were familiar. The name Schmidt was there. *Oh, right, the one who comes in to pick up supplies since Bayern usually doesn't anymore. The nurses could come here,* he thought, *to supervise or whatever.* "Alright, is everyone here now?

Once everyone was together, "Alright," Miller said to all eleven of his employees present. "We need to find space for the Harley to keep it safe, the exercise bike, a big chair or a couch and that CPM thing he's going to need. And a table. This is all according to his doctor as I am nominated as Jimmy's "health-care advocate." I'm putting him on helping the bookkeeper." He looked at Susan. "That's you. You teach him. He's off deliveries, but will be running the register and customer service. For three months on a barstool or from a lower chair with his leg up.

Mrs. Kinney, of course, had her arms folded, glaring fire and looking ready to trebuchet bombs.

Miller asked, "Mrs. Kinney—Marlene—do you have something to add?"

Her eyes narrowed, she growled, "He's taken my job! That no-good loathsome bastard!"

Miller spoke bitterly. "About that. You are doing deliveries within Grantville and out to Rudolstadt, up to Jena, and down to the military base in Saalfeld, and maybe to the stockyard. This is for three months, five months, maybe for the next decade. You will connect with our clients, providing superior customer service. It's high time you got a promotion and a raise, oh, and a percentage. You need to learn the routes, and the whole business, as Jimmy can't do anything like that right now. Waldo will go on all the runs with you, as he's also learning the whole business. He's an expert shot."

He glanced over at Waldo, then said, "I will remind young Herr Waldo, Frau Kinney is the head of your team, and you are her assistant for the hardware business and *only* that."

Young Herr Waldo gave Miller a look of disconcerted confusion. "Okay, boss, whatever you say."

Miller asked, "Okay. Now? Any questions?"

Mrs. Kinney went from screaming fire to looking totally messed with. "You're kidding, right? I'm over sixty!"

Miller shot back, "I don't freaking care anymore, Marlene. You are not old, at least not that old. I do *not* want you messing with Wild. I want you to use your energy to connect with *positive* client interaction. Not just delivery, superior service as you know everything about everyone already. You will be on the road most of the time."

She glared at him.

Miller thought, *Good. Let her be mad.* He quietly spoke, "I sent an announcement to *The Grantville Times* and *The Street.* Both papers are posting the announcement today."

"You, *what*!" Mrs. Kinney screeched at Miller. Her face got red.

He cleared his throat, "It's either that or I have you arrested for assaulting Wild by making an ice pond in front of this store. At least eight people saw you doing it. You're lucky it was him who fell and not someone else. Think of the liability! Do you really want me to tell him that? Vengeance is not pretty, nor are consequences. Considering that it was not him..."

Mrs. Kinney's face was bright red. She was breathing hard.

Everyone stared at her.

"We'll not discuss this further, will we?" Miller said.

Jena, Professor Wettin's Home
March 5, 1636, Morning

Linda Joan Jolliffe (Wild) Wettin sat at the breakfast table, her back to the eastern light streaming warmly into the room. She imagined summer from the warmth, longed for the lushness of it.

Linda flipped through her lately-delivered-days-late newspaper, *The Street.* She thought about that planned sociology major she'd walked away from. It'd been the year Linder was made and born and the terribly difficult recovery. Jimmy made it so violently worse.

Linda considered her role as the wife of physician Peter Wettin. He was a *hochadel*, she was not. *We married...the navigations since! Teaching nursing classes has run away from me, too.*

Then, there was her role of stepmother to Peter's five living children from his late wife. The youngest, Maria-Louisa, was mid-way through being four. She had to be as fair as possible to the children. Her role as mother to their two babies was also socially significant. Her role as mother to the Wild boys, both running toward manhood, was just as important. Her sons were getting old enough for marriage alliance consideration. The Wettins wanted that. So she sat on her imaginary tripod and thought it out. Keeping up with Grantville was not so much a guilty pleasure, even. She *needed* to know what was happening.

Linda opened her copy of *The Street* from Monday, March 3, 1636. She'd tackled the crossword puzzle before breakfast, before the children had come, had breakfasted on eggs, bacon, and French-style baguettes with butter and jam. She'd drunk her coffee well-sugared and with actual cream in it. She'd enjoyed the presence of her older sons and stepchildren at breakfast, hugged and kissed them, at least those who wanted kisses, on their way out to school. Of all of the seven oldest children, she had breakfast with the oldest as always. The chatter was non-stop, running to German more than English, sounding happy. The relationship with the younger children was much better than with the older ones. Her oldest stepson was just a year behind Linder, so the three boys were always together. They went to the brand-new Jena University High School, a two-year preparation program modeled after the high school in Grantville, with about six hundred students. Both of her boys were highly motivated. Her older stepson was studying to place out of several medical school classes; the younger was not yet ready.

She'd been pleased to kiss her newest little children good morning, then send them back off to play in the nursery supervised by the two nannies. *Peter takes such good care of us all!*

Alone, finally, while on her second cup of coffee, she opened and read the business section.

* * *

The Street, **March 3, 1636**

Afternoon Edition, Business Section Announcements

Miller's Hardware announced today that Frau Marlene Coonce-Kinney has been appointed manager of commercial sales. Mrs. Kinney is known for her expertise in customer relations and making sure everything is done absolutely right. Mr. Miller, CEO of Miller's Hardware, had this to say: "This promotion has been a long time in process. Mrs. Kinney is very good at her professional level. This position is a very hands-on move for her."

Miller's Hardware also announced today that Herr James A. Wild has been appointed assistant to the chief bookkeeper of...

* * *

Linda set down her coffee, gagged, coughed, "Jimmy is doing what?"

Her husband strolled into the breakfast room as she was exclaiming.

The breakfast room's layout let the light stream in beautifully, making the carved natural maple furniture glow like a Maxfield Parrish painting Linda had a poster of, framed, in her study. Peter kissed her on her cheek as he always did if any of the children might be about. It was modesty, she knew. He looked over at the headline which was causing her so much distress.

Peter sighed, "I spoke with Herr Miller." He looked exasperated.

Startled, Linda looked up at him, eyes wide. "You what?"

"Yes. Again. I went over to the liaison office, called Herr Miller after setting the radio appointment last week. I'm sure I mentioned..."

Linda flushed, angrily. "Why? There's a no-contact agreement with Jimmy. It was bad enough that Leahy Medical contacted us."

Peter calmly said, "True. But not with Herr Miller. I may have contact with the gentleman; you may even contact him if you need to."

Linda shuddered. "Jimmy has a very bad temper. Hard fists."

He nodded. Peter appreciated Linda's distress, she could see that. He reached out and touched her hand, stroking a little. "He's still having physical problems. The knee he broke in the fall on the ice was the same leg he injured in the Somalia action in the up-time."

Linda pulled back her hand. "I know. I know. Alright, but what that has to do with us—is another thing."

He sighed. Kissed her again, more intently.

Kissing him back, she paused and asked, "Did you ever apologize to those nurses? You should if you have not."

"No. You think I should?"

Linda said, resolutely, "We don't need bad blood with Grantville over my ex-husband's injuries or other issues. He has—other issues, too many. We cannot afford to burn any bridges."

Peter shrugged. "Hmm. Let me think about it. What has our cook made for our breakfast today?"

Linda said evenly, "He's outdone himself: eggs, bacon, baguettes! And, dearest, you have an orange from the orangery. We even have marmalade for the toast."

Peter smiled, beamed. "You are so good!"

Linda relaxed into that glimmer and smiled back.

He leaned in for another kiss which went on to oh-so-tingly.

Leahy Medical and Miller's Hardware
March 6, 1636, Late Afternoon

There'd been no regular supply-closet person. Shift Head Nurse Dorothea Bayern, frustrated, had delegated it to Barbie a while back, handing her the inventory forms. The big sticking point was the instrument trays—Barbie realized she was short a dozen. They'd been there, having been used, cleaned, then put away in *that* supply closet. At this inventory, they weren't anywhere, not even in the scullery.

Sometimes people took important objects as souvenirs, an irritating activity.

Dorothea said, "A courier is too expensive! Call Miller's, they've got spares. Then go and get!"

Barbie nodded and called Miller's. The phone rang fifteen times, twice. Then it was picked up by someone laughing and slammed down. When she called yet again, no one picked up. Dorothea took her patient, and making wavy motions at Barbie, told her to go.

Barbie hurried up to the covered bus stop in front of the hospital. The rise up to the highway, painted in a fresh coat of snow, was still slick, even though sanded. Her uptime workman's boots—rescued from the shop over at Rainbow Plaza a few years back—had those nice ridgy non-skid soles, preventing her from slipping excessively.

She got to the little bus shelter at the edge of the Leahy Medical property and Route 250. The shelter's sunny yellow frame was roofed and properly big enough to wait under. The yellow horse-drawn bus, one of a number running from Grantville to as far as Rudolstadt, arrived when she did. Barbie climbed up the steps and dropped her dime in the slot, taking no notice of the driver, who might have been anyone. Barbie never paid mind to the drivers. All the seats were taken, so she stood in the aisle next to a bench seat occupied by a young woman and several small children. The *kinder* were all behaving nicely for the minute, the five of them fairly well dressed, clearly excited by the ride. Barbie smiled slightly.

The bus rattled toward down-town over the icy road. Once in town, at the corner of West Main and Market Street Barbie climbed down the narrow bus steps into the crowded streets. It was getting colder. Barbie hurried to Miller's Hardware, an up-time building, unmistakable. From riding the train, she knew it had a loading dock out back, facing the rail. The front of the store was all tall and heavy glass windows. People still came to gawk at those. There was a faint crack in the door's glass that hadn't been there when she'd last gone. The hardware store was bright inside. As she opened the door, a little bell rang, echoing.

Barbie hurried to the long sales counter toward the center-back of the sales floor. There were two registers, one a genuine antique from the 1890s, she'd been told, the other not so old, maybe from the 1970s. The counter was slick white with sparkles and ground-in grunge, edged in fake-looking wood. On it was a pile of cash and coins, at least a month's pay.

This is crazy. Where is everyone? I need to do this order. Frau Böhm needs my help with the orphans tonight and the next week. Melanie Richards asked for me specifically, and there's a warm bed. It's not too far from here.

At the counter she hesitated. *This is too quiet, too empty.* Barbie hollered, "Anybody here? Anybody here?" Nothing. *Maybe they're in the back?* She hit the bell on the counter, making it jingle twice, then hit it again.

The door to the office was shut crookedly. Something scratched, tapped. Not loudly. She blinked.

Barbie called out, "Can anyone hear me?" Then yelled it in German just to be sure. Amideutsch was next. She paused, waited.

There was a muffled cry, then tapping sounds like finger tips on metal.

Barbie did not panic. Running away like she had in Magdeburg in 1631 was not an option. This was Grantville, almost five years since. Whatever was happening was happening and she was there for it. Barbie tried the door into the back, jammed tight and crooked. She considered, tried again, turning the knob, thinking, *Just crooked, not locked?* The door did not move.

She pounded on the door, yelled into the warehouse, "Can you hear me?"

A loud resounding hammering sound came from the floor behind the door.

Barbie could wiggle the door, but it was as if it was being held shut.

Something tapped her boot, startling her. Looking down, it was half a man's hand, fingers poking out from under the door, palm down, with scarcely space to move. Barbie dropped down on her knees, trying to peek under the door, but not seeing much. The space might have been two inches, likely less. It was dark. She asked, "Are you hurt?"

The man's voice came soft, scratchy, like he'd been yelling a while. He growled out, "I don't freaking know!"

She said, "Okay."

He groaned, like a man giving up, "I can't get out from under this damn thing."

The man's voice was familiar. She asked, slowly, realizing he might be the man she'd snubbed at the bar, "What damn thing?"

"It's freaking heavy!"

"Oh. Give me a minute. Are you on your abdominals?"

He moaned. "No, shit."

Barbie stood up. It was obvious the door opened inward to the rooms beyond so it was an inside room, which meant the hinges were not accessible from her side. The mere idea that the door was crooked was part of it. This was a hardware store. There were tools. Her father had some carpentry skills and she'd watched him, long ago. "I'm going to jiggle the door. Tell me what happens." She jiggled the door. "What did the jiggle do?"

"Nothing. The stupid damn table is against it."

So, she thought, *not a solution.* "Is there a back door?"

The man said, "It's probably locked or blocked or something, considering what happened here."

"Considering? What? I'll go look. Be back in a flash, okay? Where are the pry-bars?"

He said, "Please! Hurry. They're on aisle four."

Barbie dashed, grabbed a pry-bar from the stack. The pry-bar's weight and cold black metal made it formidable. She stopped at the door and yelled at it, "I'm going outside," but didn't wait to hear anything.

Barbie hurried around the side of the building nearest the railroad tracks. There was a small parking lot to navigate, no cars, just a pickup truck which looked locked. The loading dock was just beyond.

Normally there'd be other vehicles here. Normally there would even be a couple of hands to watch over the horse carts, if there had been any. Normally there'd be at least six people working, maybe more. It was as if someone had spread the word that something was going to happen. Barbie's heart raced.

Everything outside the rail-side of the hardware store was coated with...paint, tar, and from the smell, manure. What wasn't was tipped over or broken. From the look, it was very recently vandalized. She looked over to the train tracks, not cleared of snow yet...*The train is yet to get here...this afternoon.*

She yelled, "Who in the hell did this!" She was alone. She looked at the snow, sets of footprints everywhere, racing each other. As if this vandalizing was a childish game.

Barbie stood, staring, reading the graffiti, the paint splashed on the whole side of the building. It was all graffiti, all obscenities—some scrawled in particularly bad German, one word standing out a dozen times, *Strichmädchen*. An up-time construct, she knew that much. Hure, hurren, *would be our timeline, so who did this?* Barbie did not try to read any more, looked away. Couldn't imagine who it referred to. Or why Miller's business was the target.

Another scrawl caught her eye. *Betrüger, Betrüger. Du bist eine Plage für uns alle. Du bist nur für die Hölle geeignet.*

Barbie thoughts roiled. *Insults? What happened here? Herr Miller is honest, good, isn't he? This spoil of graffiti says elsewise? Is this even about Miller?* She tried figuring out the randomness of the piles of spilled building supplies everywhere. At least several people must have done this thing, as boot-shod prints ran everywhere. *The Millers have a good reputation, why should anyone sully it?*

Barbie walked towards the roll-down door. *That window is too high-up to see in.* The slightly rusted metal gate was down, locked in place. *That,* she thought, *is the warehouse, it's locked against the weather.* Someone had tried to break the gate. Barbie stomped against the cold, still holding the pry-bar. The side door next to the big roller door appeared to be a solid metal piece with a peep at eye level. *Look at all that debris on the pavement! You can't just walk into the back door. Wait.* She stood still, heart beating hard. Barbie thought, *But it is the choice. Wait. The door's ajar, popped out.* She reached out to touch the metal door. It was frosted with ice particles and dented in the middle. It was as if it had been slammed with a heavy object. Barbie thought....*They tried to use a truck.* She turned 'round, looked at the ground. *Tire tracks...lots of footprints.* She looked back at the battered truck, thinking, *Oh, my.*

The low pile of broken concrete blocks, pavers, and bricks deliberately spilled over in front of that banged-up side door, nearly everywhere on and around the loading dock. *This tells a story,* she thought, *I can't read it.* There were piles of other supplies, normally neatly stacked—she was certain—spilled. Barbie climbed over the pile in the other direction.

She was able to get closer to the door and its peephole. On closer inspection, the peephole was smeared with paint, still drippy-looking. Barbie touched it lightly, pulled back and rubbed her fingers together...sticky, red, meant to resemble blood. She yelled through the open slit, "Can you hear me?"

The man's raspy voice called softly, "Yes!"

She heard him, called out, "How long have you been stuck?"

There was a painful groan. "Two hours, maybe."

"Well, Miller's back door is sticky with paint, it has a pile of those concrete bricks blocking it and other stuff. They look like they spilled over. I can move them."

The pained voice continued, "Please be careful. I don't think those fell over on their own."

"I will. I'm going to go call for help."

Once inside and at the front counter, again, Barbie dialed the emergency number at the fire station, appreciative of whoever had painted it on the counter. She gave the name and address of the hardware store to the man on the other end of the phone line.

The man's warm voice, familiar, said someone should be there shortly. He asked, "Where's everyone else?"

Barbie said, "Are you Estes Frost? I don't know where everyone is! I came to order something for Leahy. I'm going back to the side to see if I can move those pavers."

"No, I'm not Frost, but he'll be there soon. If traffic cooperates. Be careful."

"I will." She clicked off the phone.

Barbie went back to the side of Miller's Hardware. She carefully started the process of undoing the pile in front of the side door. Barbie restacked the jumbled pavers to the side. She moved about two dozen pavers, stopped, and rested. Yelled into the warehouse, "Are you alright?"

The man's raspy voice croaked out, "I guess."

Barbie called back, "Okay! Your throat must be sore." She thought, *two hours or more, maybe, squashed like a bug? Why would anyone do this?* In a short time she removed enough of the scattered concrete blocks and pavers so that the exterior door became movable. She called out. "There's space!"

"Do what you can," came the mumbly croak.

Barbie wiggled the door. It moved a little better. Finishing the rest was just as difficult. "Everything's heavy. Almost in," she hollered. She had a two-foot pull-out space. She took a deep breath, then squeezed inside, carrying the pry bar. She called out, "It's dark. I have a pry bar."

The voice grumped hoarsely, "Yep. Light switch is to the door's right. Feel for it, toggle it. It...it's stubborn, it sometimes won't go on."

The light flicked on and buzzed. Barbie looked up to the old fluorescents above. One of them buzzed, flickered, then held steady. The buzz stopped.

The voice rasped, "Thank you—hurry!"

Miller's Hardware warehouse was packed to the roof with goods and tools—it was a treasure house. The shelving was over twelve feet tall and nearly as wide as a man was long, maybe more. There were a lot of rows like that. Barbie passed a couple of paint mixer stations, then full racks of paint cans and barrels. There were boxes of colorizers marked as coming from Lothlorien, the Stones. As she walked forward in the direction of the front of the hardware store the soft tap tap of her boots was loud enough to echo.

The warehouse was dimly lit. She looked up again. Some of the lights above showed their ages. Where the fluorescents were gone, there were the Edison lights, big and disconcertingly yellow, not easy on the eyes.

The door to the offices was broken in from the warehouse side. She stood there for a minute, looking. On the left there was a weight lifting machine and an exercise bike, looking well-used. There was a machine lying on the sofa, an odd thing really, small, as long as a man's leg. Barbie remembered it was called a CPM; it'd been an object of fascination for a few days at Leahy. On the right of the office there was a desk, a battered thing much used and not particularly well-cared for. She whispered, "Where are you?"

There was no reply. There were faded sirens in the distance. It seemed like it'd been forever since the phone call.

Barbie found and flicked on another light switch, making the offices a bit brighter and leaving a greasy residue on her fingers. She glanced at them and wiped the blood on her skirt.

She moved faster. Table legs stuck out sideways, the rest seemed crunched, axed. A man's legs poked out from under the table, not crushed. One of his legs was in an up-time binder designed to steady broken bones. She knew it to have metal stays and velcro. *It is the guy from the bar under there!* "Where is your head?"

"I'm stuck under this...on my stomach," he said, "there's just enough space."

"I've called emergency services, the paramedics. You're right, this is jamming the door."

"I'm Jimmy," he moaned, "Thank you. When did they say they were coming?"

"I know you, I think. They'll be here soon, I expect. Where is everyone, Jimmy?"

"I'm not sure. I was pretty much by myself this afternoon. I got in this morning. Mrs. Kinney left with Waldo to deliver some orders to Saale. A couple of others, not their day. I expect Jenn is at home, and Barlowe." He hesitated, "Ben left after, just boogied. I never saw Joe this morning. I don't know who went with Ben. Never said anything to me. A couple of people were talking about The Hole in the Wall. And Daph is home with a sick kid, she only drops off the kid so Marlene has an excuse to leave early."

Barbie said quietly, "That crazy place with the parrot room? The wolf?"

"Yep. That crazy place. Hmm. Normally there are like four of us here, maybe five. Mr. Miller went somewhere this morning before I got in, so he's not here. He was supposed to be back already."

She dropped to her knees, "Alright," she said. "But that doesn't explain this. And that table must be really heavy."

Jimmy said, "Yep. I'm not sure how to explain this. I can't wiggle out, my knee is in this immobilizer and I am not supposed to move it the way I need to. It hurts too much."

Barbie said, "You need to breathe more. This could be a crush injury."

"I don't feel crushed."

"Okay."

Jimmy exhaled, "You're a nurse. Are you Barbie Schmidt? I remember you from the hospital. This situation is stupid. I always have stupid stuff happen."

"Yes, I'm Barbie. I'm here, not going anywhere. So, what happened, Jimmy?"

He was quiet. "You know the wolf guy? That story?"

"I was there, remember?"

"Oh, yeah. Oh, oh, you're the girl with the red cloak...and the pretty hair. I can see the edge of your cloak."

She giggled.

His voice relaxed, "Barbie. Okay. That guy, Rudolph Jaegerson, came into the store first. You know, the one who was hunting that wolf pack back on the night of February 6th. We—he and I—got four of them eventually, that night. They were huge. Not the whole pack, mind you. I thought he wanted to talk about going after more of the wolves. He, that guy, asked if I knew anything about Miller's safe."

"Humm. Isn't a safe normal for a business?"

"Yep. It's not normal for a customer to inquire about the contents of a safe. That was...odd. Miller has a couple of safes, three I think, but I don't have the combinations or anything. Not my business. Miller only opens any one of them when it needs to be opened, otherwise they're locked and in a locked room. I don't know what he keeps in any of them, except they're not empty. The one they wanted is important to Carlos Villareal. Miller's keeping something for him, like for years."

"Oh," she said, "didn't he...isn't he a jeweler?"

"He's a rockhound. He travels a lot when he's not tending the bar at the Thuringen Gardens. Or teaching geology at the high school."

Barbie thought it through. "Doesn't matter this minute. How are you doing?"

The sounds of sirens abruptly stopped, both sets. There was the sound of running feet, a lot of them in the store. Jimmy shouted, "We're back here!"

She yelled, "Come around the side!"

Jimmy then said to Barbie quietly, "I declined to help Rudolph Jaegerson as the safes are not my business. About the same time another guy walked in, a down-time man. I've never seen him before. He called me 'Herr Kinney,' which is weird in a disgusting sort of way."

"That is odd. What if he didn't know your name?"

"The first guy did not correct him. Let it ride. I was not expecting that. But the first guy said a name, umm, umm, Jökullsson, maybe. I wasn't clear on what was happening. The Jökullsson dude dumped a whole pile of gold coins and paper on the front counter. Then asked about the Kinney *Straßenmädchen*."

Barbie said, "The money is there. Why would they ask that...horrible thing?"

Jimmy said, "Long story. Leave the money, it's gotta be dirty. So I asked, what for? Then the wolf-hunter guy rushed me and grabbed me. He shoved me towards the back wall. I did a pit on him, got him into a take-down lock. I tried to throw him down. Then the second guy punched me in the face before I could finish, so I punched him back, hit him once. Then, he punched me, again, a bunch. So, like a fool, I stepped back to run, if I could. The first guy grabbed me from the side. The last thing I really remember is someone's knee in my back, something that felt like a baseball bat to my side and I woke up under this sideways table two hours ago. But I don't think it's only two guys. There were more. I heard at least two other voices."

"But you have no idea?"

"Nope. I can feel my toes so nothing important is broken. I just hurt. Is the safe alright? I mean, it *is* bolted to the concrete."

"I don't know, Jimmy. I'm not looking. I'm talking to you. Not looking to carry more bricks, you know."

He laughed bitterly.

The ambulance siren screamed its presence just outside the warehouse, then the siren stopped. A gritty sliding noise on the snow and ice happened next, like it was right next to the outside wall.

After the briefest moment, there came the familiar noise of squawking doors creaking open and feet stomping the ground. The crunch of bolt cutters rolled through the warehouse from outside. Woven in and around were many people's voices. It sounded like a whole lot of emergency people coming for just one man's aid.

There was a grating sound. A rattle from outside. A shimmery lifting crunch sound, glass breaking, then the slide-up door moving. Barbie had already cued it, walking swiftly out of the office towards the back, yelling "We're here!"

Jimmy yelled, "Hurry!"

The group of paramedics and firemen rushed forward. Barbie noted Rothrock and Brother Girard from the firehouse—she saw them often enough. The others were just nameless faces to her. Estes Frost, the police officer, strode in, and took over, directing people.

It took four of the men to lift the table, then drag it some feet away.

Miller's home-made concrete-block-and-wood bookcase had been tipped over. The red steel fishing tackle box spilled out beyond that. A pry-bar was hooked under the door's lever handle, stuck behind a cast-iron pipe on one side. The other edge of the pry bar was hooked up against the door's middle hinge. Barbie did not see how, just that it was.

The paramedics carefully lifted Jimmy onto a backboard, then the gurney, then settled him in the ambulance.

A barrel of flammable materials, petrol, that hadn't gone off was found last, in a corner down the paint aisle. It showed no signs of attempts at being lit. There was a dripping bloody handprint on it, man-sized.

Leahy Medical Center
March 6, 1636, Evening

Jimmy hated cops on principle. The police had left him a few minutes back, after asking too many questions, calling it a "statement," bothering him. He'd had too much trouble learning how not to be an idiot or somebody's whipping boy, usually both. Out of the corner of his eye, which he'd just barely flicked open, he saw Doc Adams enter.

"I know you're awake," Doc Adams said.

Jimmy, on his back, definitively opened his eyes and stared at the ceiling, counting those stupid-looking white acoustic ceiling tiles. He said finally, "I do not like cops."

Doc Adams said, "They finished their questioning. Let's talk about something else. You do know you can't go home right now? You've bruising consistent with a self-defensive fight. We ran you under the X-ray at the vet's, just to be sure. Those X-rays we managed to get show no new breaks. Your knee is not messed up any worse."

"But no more breaks?"

"Nope. However, you have a black eye, the bruised cheek running purple and green just under it, another large bruise on your lower back, running to your right side. Someone hit you with what looks like a baseball bat or a table leg. And a sprained shoulder."

He exhaled, "Okay. Do I get more painkillers?"

"Aspirin. Only aspirin, you know why. No alcohol for two weeks. And three days in the hospital, five days at home."

"Crap. Oh, crap! Oh, crap! No need. I know it." Jimmy laughed until he hiccupped and couldn't stop laughing and hiccupping.

Doc Adams exclaimed, "Easy! This is *not* funny."

"You're right, it is a damned situational irony. All I can have is aspirin due to my ancient history which someone finally remembered! So what now? Who's responsible for those dimwits trying to get me to open Mr. Miller's safes?" Jimmy hiccupped again.

Doc Adams exhaled. "We don't know."

When Jimmy laughed some more, it was bitter. "Does Mr. Miller know?"

"Yes, he does," Doc Adams said. "He's, I suppose, sorting it all out. He said he ran to Saale this morning to get a document signed, lots of weird shit happened. He's here, ask him."

Some minutes later Ken Miller stalked in, rolling on anger hardly contained, a notebook under his arm. "Wild, I am so sorry. I was delayed. Someone stole my truck, ran it into the river. I had to buy a damn horse to get back here. You look like hell. Those men, they beat you to within an inch of your life."

Jimmy, relieved when he saw Miller, said almost at the same moment, "You're not hurt, that's good. Is the truck salvageable?"

Miller nodded, "Maybe. It didn't sink. We retrieved it pretty fast."

Jimmy whistled, "Wow. I remember some, boss, but not everything."

"Okay. Go over everything you remember with me. As if I were needing to know the slightest details. Bit by bit. I'm taking notes."

* * *

Much later, at home, Miller looked over the police report. It was about as complete as anyone might get. It was not a terribly convoluted report, just an incomplete carbon copy.

Jimmy Wild was quite distressed about, well, everything. The man did have a conscience. He tried to give everything he could about the *event*. Obviously, some information was lacking on Wild's part. He hadn't noticed everything.

Miller leaned back in his desk chair, grumbling. Tracing anything like this was going to be a problem. It wasn't as if you could go and confront the bad guys; that only happened in the movies. *But I have a name for that man, Jökullsson. Something to go on, now.*

Miller sighed. Jimmy Wild was alive. He hadn't been crushed to death, *thank God.* Miller knew he'd not find out anything further on his own about the men involved, presuming it was only men. *I've heard of someone, a math teacher from high school. Hmmm. Good with solving odd problems? Who is it? Simons, Leslie, or Esslie? Who'd know? It's not like Ditmar Schaub is around to ask. Maybe I should ask Rothrock. He knows a lot of people. Marlene was out of town, so, hmmph. Not her, not likely. This is gonna cost so much time.*

Grantville Times, **Established September MDCXXXI**
Afternoon Edition, Friday, March 7, 1636
Herr Lyle Kindred, Publisher

Grantville Man Attacked in Miller's Hardware Store While Stopping a Burglary

Byline Herr Otto Martin

Herr James Wild, 38, of Grantville, was doing his due diligence at work when he was approached by Rudolph Jaegerson of Rudolstadt and asked for access to a safe on the premises. There was another man with Jaegerson, name unknown.

According to Mr. Miller, the safe is not in use as it is not practical, nor has it been for at least a decade as the lock is solidly rusted shut.

Herr Miller had been called down to Saalfeld...

Jimmy's Place
March 15, 1636, Late Afternoon

Having locked up his singlewide, Jimmy got ready to get down the stairs. Going up was a basic reverse.

Jimmy long since figured out the procedure to get down his stairs. He was proud of that. All it took was a bit of ingenuity to slide down the outside stairs at his place. Someone had wrapped the handrail in rope before he'd got out of the hospital. That was nice. He'd been in the immobilizer for about a month. Had another month to go. Then three more months of the brace, walking with a cane. Jimmy had gotten a crumbly leather-clad office chair which could raise and lower, still. He stood balanced on one foot as carefully as he could, folded up the walker, dropped it on the porch deck. He then carefully set down onto the chair and hit the lever. He dropped to within six inches of the deck, then let himself down to the cold wood of that deck. He grabbed the folded walker, slid it down first. He followed, bumping down the steps with a degree of caution.

Jimmy stood carefully, leaning on the opened walker, injured leg stuck out, resting on his heel under three layers of wooly socks. *Patience pays,* he thought. *Hunger, that's another matter. Nothing to eat in the house. Nothing I want. So. It's not as cold as a month back. The snow is almost at the beginning of the spring melt.* It was still cold enough to make a white plume in the air when he exhaled. He waited patiently for his ride.

Old Fred pulled up. His mighty steeds—as the old man would say—were their usual feisty happy selves, as old war horses often were. Some things

Old Fred had said to Jimmy made it obvious that the man's English was much better than he let on. He drove passengers all over Grantville and sometimes to Rudolstadt. His horse cart had steps just the right height for Jimmy to manage, so it was a no-brainer to use the services. He climbed in and sat next to Fred like always, folded up the walker, didn't look to the back. Like always.

Old Fred asked, "*Wo willst du denn essen*, Herr Wild?"

Jimmy said, "I need a dinner, Old Fred." Then he added, awkwardly, "Um, *Ich brauche ein gutes Abendessen.*"

Old Fred laughed, saying in heavily accented English, "Your German is bad, Wildman!"

Jimmy side-eyed. "Oh."

"I know, I know, saying it, *that's* hard." Old Fred laughed. "*Deinem Knie geht es besser, richtig?*"

Jimmy grinned, cleared his throat. "It, it is. Thank you for asking."

"*Denken Sie daran, dass die Dinge hier nicht immer so sind, wie sie scheinen.*" He paused then said, "*Mit Ihnen werde ich Englisch sprechen. Für andere werde ich es nicht tun. Für alles gibt es Gründe.* As I do know you are not stupid, you have learnt to get by in German if you need to. Do not be uncertain. As for your knee, it will continue to get better. I hear you are working hard on that."

He chortled a little, "That still leaves dinner. Who told you that my knee is getting better?"

Old Fred looked over at him, laughing, "Yes. It has been said. You like Hole in the Wall?"

"They're decent."

"That they are."

The short rest of the ride was fairly silent. The horses, of course, made sounds back to Old Fred, who nickered at them kindly. It was as if he actually understood them. The Hole in the Wall loomed brightly, welcoming. Old Fred pulled up the horse cart, stopping neatly. Jimmy paid the man and managed to disembark from the horse cart relatively well, putting his walker in front of him to lean on.

There was new front decking on the porch into The Hole in the Wall, a new jute welcoming all-weather woven mat lay in front of the doors. There were a couple of warm-weather benches sitting outside. There were the double doors, which looked like they always had, politely over-used. Like confident deer, several sets of people came and went in before Jimmy even got up on the porch. It took a hot minute to deal with the steps but Jimmy did climb the steps, struggling with his balance. The walker made that clipping sound that walkers were wont to. Jimmy almost did not notice the sound; he'd gotten that used to it long since

Someone held one of the doors for him, and he mumbled, "Thank you." Once inside, he scanned the room automatically, saw a familiar-looking dark red cloak towards the back of the pool tables, then lost the view.

Jimmy wanted a beer before anything else. The tap, tap of his walker sounded louder than the music, which was that Kidz Bop version of "Macarena," again. The song cut off, then changed over to "One Night in Bangkok" as he clipped up to the bar, folded and leaned the walker safely, then gingerly climbed on the barstool. The parrots in the parrot room were bobbing their heads, screeching and cursing in time with the music in at least five languages.

Rothrock was at the bar. The man asked him, "Beer?"

Jimmy said like any wit, with a bite, "Might as well. Rothrock, you're still slumming? Who's spinning the music?"

Rothrock laughed. "Pays some bills. The Jenss boys are spinning tonight, Anton and Ludwig, they're here often enough. The nurses are here." He grinned.

Jimmy raised an eyebrow, laughed, "Really? After what happened the last time I was here?" He became slightly aware that someone stood next to him as he balanced on the barstool. "So. What's good on the menu?"

Rothrock, a distracted look on his face, said, "You had the cabbage rolls last time. I only remember it as that night went so crazy, the wolf and all."

A woman's voice next to Jimmy said, "Two plates of that and a pitcher of beer. The Wildman is not sitting on a stool and eating. His nurse does not approve of a barstool. He'll have supper with us. I've seen his knee bones in surgery, Rothrock, that qualifies as a huge no on barstool sitting!"

He turned slightly. "Barbie," he said.

"Jimmy," she said, "you're joining us tonight, right?"

"There's a place for me?"

"We'll make space if you stop staring at me!"

He smiled slightly. "Sure. Why not?"

"You're doing it again," she said. But she laughed.

* * *

Rothrock stood behind the bar, watching. Jimmy maneuvered across the floor, going around pool tables and people. It was like a dance really, keeping in time with Barbie Schmidt, click-clicking the walker past the pool tables while the players' balls clacked off the rims of the tables. He saw Jimmy's slight limp even with the walker. *Maybe not as bad as before.* The song in the background switched up to "Holding Out For a Hero." Rothrock reflected on the Jenss boys' taste in up-time music.

That table was packed with the herd of nurses and some of the orderlies. Barbie helped Wild get seated without letting him fall over. She put him right next to her. One of the other nurses leaned the walker against a nearby roof support post.

In a few minutes, the entire party was served, their dinners set before them. The rest of the herd of nurses and orderlies chatted away, almost encircling Wild. He didn't come across as a wolf, even in sheep's clothing.

Rothrock noted that Barbie was lively and chattery with the Wildman. He couldn't hear anything above the conversations, the clack of the pool balls on the white enameled tables, and the persistent music in the background. It was all part of the beat of the scene.

Granted, he thought, *the Wildman can be quite well-mannered. He's a survivor. Johannes Esslie is not going to like this at all. I am not telling him. Johannes told me Barbara Schmidt was dead in old Magdeburg until five months back. He saw her for the first time, then, even though she's lived here for years. They don't move in the same circles. Never noticed each other. He saw her coming out of a surgical room at Leahy. She did not see him.* A song he'd not heard before played in the background, the words started with "Sweet Dreams."

There were peals of laughter over something funny at the nurses' table. Rothrock didn't hear it, just saw the laughter. Jimmy actually looked happy. His eyes were crinkled and he seemed to be hooting a good laugh. *These up-timers are different,* Rothrock mused.

Jimmy passed a buttered slice of black bread to Barbie.

She took a bite, laughed, clearly said, "That's salty!!"

Jimmy laughed back. At that point they twined wrists and each took a sip of the other's beer.

Rothrock thought, *That's interesting.* He got distracted. There were orders to take and a bar to manage. The song switched to "The Sound of Silence."

Some new people came into The Hole in the Wall, letting the cold chew into the barroom. Someone said, in passing, "The moon is in the first quarter..."

Someone else chirped on their way out, "Jupiter lies west..."

Those damned parrots in the parrot room next to the bar started scream-ing the song lyrics, then cursing, then singing "The Sound of Silence."

Rothrock sighed. *The spies are back*, he thought. He turned back to look at the customers at the bar. He noticed Old Fred looking at him, motioning.

He stepped over. "What can I get for you?"

Old Fred said, "I'd like a beer, Herr Rothrock. And a favor."

"A beer is eminently doable. Would you be interested in some Augustin-er Bräu München?"

Old Fred seemed to give the small matter a degree of consideration, "Ah, I would. And, what Jimmy the Wildman is having for his dinner?"

"Of course." Rothrock stepped away for a moment, opened the kitchen door, called in, returned, and poured the beer. "What can I do for you, Old Fred?"

"You see the Wildman with that young woman? She calls herself Barbara Schmidt? The nurse?"

"So? That's her name."

"Hmmph," he seemed to reflect. "No, not entirely. Make sure they stay together. For both their happinesses."

"I don't see how I can do anything."

Old Fred sighed. "Barbara Schmidt survived Magdeburg, yes?"

"As I understand it. Yes."

Old Fred drank his beer in nearly a gulp. "Another, please."

"Of course." Rothrock poured the beer, this time a tad more generously. A plate of the hot cabbage rolls arrived with butter noodles and sauerkraut.

"Ah," said Old Fred. "Marvelous!" He ate for a bit, put down the fork—the up-time styled device that was now ordinary even down into the working classes—and drank some more beer. The song in the background switched again, to "Danger Zone."

Both men looked over across the room to the Wildman's table with the nurses. Barbie was laughing at some random thing. Jimmy Wild was sitting tight to her.

Rothrock said, blandly, "She does seem happy. You know her?"

Old Fred gave him that *look*. Drank some more beer. Ate more of the cabbage rolls. Finally said, "I knew her somewhat in Magdeburg, a proper young woman. I was relieved to see her alive here, oh maybe three years back. I am not certain if she is aware of me. I am certainly not going over to say anything." He shrugged, as if to say, *I've done my duty.* "I had thought the entire family died in the siege."

"A lot of people did. I've heard reports."

"I was there. It was far worse than the reports. These cabbage rolls are delicious."

Rothrock said carefully, "I have heard your pretty steeds are war horses."

Old Fred eyeballed him, "That they were. Quite nicely retired. I make a decent living on them. You are aware that the spies are back?"

"It seems obvious."

"Good." He paused, then quietly said, "The truth is, Barbara Schmidt is not a spy, not even a sleeper as the up-timers would have it. She is a nurse. Before that, she was brought up..." Old Fred hesitated, then said, "to marry the son of a burgher, she is of an...old family. The contract was supposed to have been signed on May 22, 1631."

"Oh. Even during the siege? More beer? Who was supposed to officiate at the signing?" Served up the beer.

Old Fred gave him that blandly cryptic look. "The siege was not expected to be an extermination effort. Life doesn't stop going on. Everything is negotiable. Trust me. Consider this, if marriage is a good deal, then it is made in Heaven and blessed by God and his angels. If it is a bad deal, then it will be Hell to pay here on Earth and ever-after."

Rothrock stared over at Jimmy and Barbie. "Oh. So, is this good?"

Old Fred nodded.

Rothrock watched as Old Fred got up and left after paying for his meal. He was disquieted. Not for the first time he wondered what he was missing. He looked back at the table. As he watched the pair, they seemed to mirror each other.

The cold air rolled in, bringing a swirl of snow.

The song in the background had gone on to "Take on Me." It was the first quarter of the New Moon. *Wait a minute,* he thought, *Old Fred is a spy?* Rothrock shook his head, *cannot be,* he decided. *And Jimmy is not alone, not any more.*

Something Old
Bethanne Kim

Author's Note:

My all-new 1632 novel *Red Shield* is being released in January 2026 by Baen Books. The story of Harry and Betty Ruth in the post-RoF world is a minor story woven into the novel. This takes place after those events, but it tells their backstory from the decades before the Ring of Fire. Fair warning: Unlike my other stories and novels, this is not a happy tale.

January 1636

Betty Ruth Snodgrass's family and friends were gathered to remember her. More accurately, her granddaughter Juliet McCabe was clearing out the last of her things from the Bowers Assisted Living Facility and Betty Ruth's friends had wandered in out of boredom, sharing stories when they thought of one.

Wiping the dust from the top of a mid-1960s shoe box her husband had spotted on top of the wardrobe, Juliet turned pink. "What was Grammie doing with a Frederick's of Hollywood catalog, let alone three of them?"

Alma cackled. "Only one thing to do with their catalogs! Buy something to have a bit of fun, girl! We figured out pretty quick after we arrived here in the seventeenth century that we should keep our junk mail. Frederick's and Victoria's Secret were both persistent with their mailing, so your Grammie still had a few around the house. Once we found out what those old Playboys went for, well, you can guess what we thought about our lingerie catalogs! Especially the ones from Frederick's. She was planning on selling one of those to take a trip to Italy with Harry next summer."

"She would've loved that. She and Harry had so much fun the last few years. It was really sweet." Juliet tugged open another drawer, shoulders sagging when she saw what was inside. "I never understood why Grammie had so many record jackets with no records. One day, I came in and she was sweeping up a smashed record. When I asked, she said it was her fault, but that's not an explanation."

Alma's face turned sad like a light switched off. "She may have said it was her fault, girl, might even have believed it, but fragile things didn't last in Abner's house and that's all I want to say about that. You remember how she helped you out with some money a few years ago? She sold the jacket for her favorite Aretha Franklin album. Now that we're talking, it reminds me. She left her Tina Turner albums in Harry and Verlinda's house and they may still be there. She bought CDs after Abner died. I'll go have the nurses call and ask Harry's family to bring her things to your house. Back in a minute. "

Flipping through the catalogs as Alma spoke, Juliet tapped them into a neat stack and set them to the side. Noticing the address on the cover, her eyes narrowed and she pointed an accusatory finger at the cover, glaring at her husband Zane. "She was keeping things at Harry's house when Grandad was still alive. And getting mail delivered there! Was Grammie cheating on Grandad? All this time I thought Grandad was the problem in that house and maybe it was Grammie cheating on him?"

She was nearly shouting, not caring who heard her saying the Grammie she loved and trusted was a homewrecking cheater who made her own home a misery and probably did the same to Harry and Verlinda Lynch's home. Putting out a hand, palm down and making lowering motions, Zane tried to get her to quiet down. "Don't jump to conclusions, hon. Maybe there's an explanation."

Juliet was having none of it. "Half the people here are so deaf they can't hear me and the rest probably already know! I'm the only one still thinking my Grammie was a good person! They already know she was a..."

Zane clapped a hand over her mouth. "Stop. Please. At least ask someone before you say worse things. Sometimes mailing lists have wrong addresses. No, I don't really believe that, but before you keep going like this, we need to have something better than 'she left records at Harry's house' and 'some catalogs were delivered there.' Ask her friends. Look at Alma standing there in the door. Honey, you shocked Alma Hawkins into silence. That's not easy to do."

Alma nodded. "He's right, but I'm not the best one to talk. You just wait right there while I get Mary Susan. She was always close to your Grammie and she's just down the hall."

Nearly shaking with anger, Juliet was gone before Alma came back with Mary Susan.

* * *

Hands shoved deep into her coat pockets, Juliet headed across the street and up the hill toward her home, once her grandparents' house. She and Zane had moved in not long after the Ring of Fire to help Betty Ruth.

Everyone agreed that in exchange, they inherited the house. The truth was the house had bad memories for everyone. Juliet and Zane were the only ones who were renting in April 2000, when they came back through time, so they were the only ones who needed a house.

The key still caught when she turned it, just like always. Something had been stuck in there longer than anyone could remember. It used to sound like bits of glass, now it just ground a little bit, more like sand. No one in the family ever talked about the bad memories, just brushed them under the rug, but it seemed like she had to think about them today. Had to air things out.

The walls were the hardest to ignore, but she'd had a lot of years to practice. Today, she forced herself to look, to *feel* what had been done. She knew the spots: took down the paintings, moved the chairs, uncovered what her family kept hidden. Her hands trailed over the rough patches done by an inexperienced hand. Her palm lay flat on another place where the repair was more skillful. Finally, she stood, staring, at one wall, trying to remember. *I saw the hole. It was there one day before Grandad went to his favorite bar, nursing his hand. I saw how bloody his knuckles were. Grammie took me for ice cream and when we got home, Aunt Marilyn was finishing cleaning up. It's like the hole was never there. But I'm sure it was.*

Grandad's old recliner was out with the trash even before his funeral. Juliet had helped pick out the new one to replace it, and that's where she sat now, staring at the doors. Not a hollow-core door to be found, and no glass panels in the front door. Nothing easily broken, just like the rest of the house. The Melamine dishes. The picture frames with no glass. The plastic glasses. There weren't even any porcelain lamps until after Grandad died, which was odd in a house that old. After a while, Juliet left silently, head bowed in thought as she trudged back to the Bowers, steps heavier than when she had rushed over.

* * *

Stopping at the reception desk, she asked them to send Alma and Mary Susan McIntire to Betty Ruth's room. As Juliet walked in, head bowed, Zane tensed in his seat, then rushed over to wrap her in a hug. He still hadn't let go when Alma and Mary Susan walked in.

Alma snorted. "Young people. Get a room! We're here, like you asked. Have you gotten over yourself a bit, young lady? You were screaming some awful things about your grandmother that sweet lady most certainly did *not* deserve."

Anger flickered in Juliet's eyes, then died. "You said Mary Susan could explain it. I'm ready to listen." Still wrapped in Zane's arms, she looked at Mary Susan. "So please, enlighten me. Tell me why my grandma had mail sent to another man's house and left her treasured things there, but it wasn't a problem."

Mary Susan McIntire walked over to the only upholstered chair in the room, her hand on Alma's to keep her steady without her walker, giving a little shake of her head. "What you were yelling wasn't fair to Betty Ruth. Alma here told me you started up that ruckus because you saw some catalogs for Betty Ruth were delivered to Harry's house, but that's not what happened. They were delivered to *Verlinda's* house. Harry didn't know, not until after Verlinda got so sick and stopped getting the mail every day. Even then, he never knew how long it had been going on. She had her Tupperware orders left there, too. Abner thought Tupperware was too expensive."

As Mary Susan settled into the comfy chair, Alma sat down on the bed. Eleanor Jenkins walked up and leaned in the doorway, quietly motioning for them to continue. Mary Susan plucked at the blanket she was sitting on, then wrapped the ends over her legs, and straightened up, resolve in her eyes. "You're a grown woman, Juliet. I don't know much about what went on in that house, but I'll tell you what I do know. First, your Grammie didn't do anything with Harry that his wife didn't know about. Harry mostly just made sure Abner knew he couldn't haul off and put Betty Ruth or the kids in the hospital with his drinking and his temper. It didn't stop everything, but it helped."

Eleanor stepped inside and quietly closed the door. "I know a bit more. She's right. Betty Ruth didn't do a thing with Harry that Verlinda didn't know about, but she did things with Verlinda that Harry didn't know about. Like the mail and packages being delivered there instead of her house and that name change of hers. It was Verlinda's idea after Abner died. Betty Ruth finally admitted, once he was gone, what a son of a bitch he was and the only good things to come from that marriage were her kids and her house.

"Sometime in '88, after your Uncle Ben died but before Verlinda passed, obviously, she finally convinced your Grammie to go ahead and change her name back to Snodgrass. She didn't have any kids named Walsh anymore, with two of 'em dead and the third married for decades. Verlinda passed before it was done, but I remember Betty Ruth showing off that new driver's license with her old name on it. She was so proud that she had done it."

In the silence that followed, Juliet thought back. She had been too busy to pay much attention at the time, but Grammie had proudly shown her the new license, too. She was much quieter now, calmer. "That doesn't explain the mail."

"Harry told Verlinda before they ever got married about Abner and Betty Ruth. That he wanted to keep Betty Ruth safe, but there was nothing more to it. The two women got to know each other and became friends, but Abner hated Harry, so Betty Ruth had to be careful. One day, Verlinda caught Betty Ruth looking at some of her catalogs when she came back from the bathroom. When she found out Abner had punched more than one hole in the wall because he disapproved of a magazine she received—Cosmo, I think—Verlinda marched Betty Ruth down to the post office and they talked to the only woman mail carrier there. She started rerouting some of Betty Ruth's mail to Verlinda's house and eventually they even changed the mailing address for some of it."

Zane and Juliet were sitting on the bed, listening, his arms still wrapped protectively around her but not as tightly. Juliet nodded, thoughtful. "If it was one of the days Grammie was wearing her big Hollywood sunglasses, that would have done it. They did a good job of hiding the shiners from straight on, but not from the sides."

Tapping a nail on her front tooth, Eleanor seemed to be weighing a decision. "There was another thing. She had a bank account. In Fairmont. In case...well, just in case. I don't think she ever knew in case of what, but it was there. And probably still is. There's some other stuff at Harry and Verlinda's old house. I'll stop by and have someone drop it by your place." Seeing the question forming, she continued, "Breakables, including her beloved Tina Turner albums, worn out as they are. It was hard to miss that the only breakable things in that house were the windows and a few mirrors. Anything else that happened with Abner is probably best left with the dead now, but"—Eleanor waved around the room—"none of us want to see you thinking those kinds of things about Betty Ruth."

Alma snorted. "But think whatever you want of Abner Walsh, as long as it's bad."

Zane asked, "Why did Harry let Abner keep giving her black eyes?"

Giving the tiniest shrug, Mary Susan answered. "Because she wouldn't leave him. Always said all those things you heard on TV. 'He doesn't mean it.' 'He's really sorry.' 'It was my fault for messing up.' But Harry made it clear there was a line Abner couldn't cross or he'd have to deal with a man hitting back, not a woman cowering in fear."

Juliet rolled her neck, tension easing out of her. "Thank you, ladies. That does help a lot. Now I need to finish packing her things, and I have some thinking to do."

February 1636

"Juliet! Honey, I'm home!" Zane walked into his kitchen to find Juliet staring at a letter, tears streaming down her cheeks. After more than a quarter century of marriage, he had never seen her cry like that. Not over anything but a person dying or coming close to it, at any rate. "Honey? What's wrong? What happened?" He kneeled and took her in his arms.

Gradually, she released the tension in her body and sat back. "The letter."

Zane nodded, knowing that if he spoke too much, it would derail her thoughts and the whole thing would take longer. "Go on, honey, I'm listening."

Juliet took a deep breath. "Mom was twenty-four when she died. I always kind of wondered about that. She was so young. Uncle Ben and Aunt Marilyn made comments about Grandad, but I never saw anything. I mean, sure they seemed to repaint the house a lot. And Uncle Ben, Aunt Marilyn, and Grammie were all good at minor home repairs, but lots of people are."

Confused, Zane nodded.

"You remember all those things they said when we cleaned out her room and then we got a few boxes of stuff from Mr. and Mrs. Lynch's house? I've been going through it. The Tina Turner albums were there and I went to put them with the other albums and the other albums were just empty jackets with nothing in them and then I looked inside and..." The gentle pressure and warmth of Zane's hand on her wrist brought her back. Deep breath. "Thank you. I was spiraling. Something made me look inside the empty record jackets from her room at the end.

"You need to read what she wrote to Harry. It was in a record sleeve from a Sinatra album, *Romantic Songs from the Early Years*. I almost missed it. Like the old ladies said, they didn't have much that was breakable in the house until after Grandad died. Here. Read it."

Dear Harry,

I remember the first time we met. Your mom hired me to babysit you even though I wasn't even six years older than you. We were up from Beckley to visit my Pa's people. Even that little, you loved anything with a ball. I wasn't surprised when you were a star on the football team.

The next time I saw you was that day. It's the only time I was ever glad the damn fool got so drunk. Bad as what you got looked, I can't deny I enjoy replaying the memory of him going down. Purely karma, as the kids today say, that he landed on his own broken bottle.

Your dad came over the next day. Did you know that? If Abner hadn't already been in the hospital, your dad would've put him there for slicing your chest up the way he did. Had the Police Chief with him and I told 'em what happened. My Marilyn was just big enough to know to hide and not make a sound when Abner got that way, but Carolyn was still little. She was crying, that's what set him off. I wasn't in the room, but he did something to her before you got there. She was never quite the same after that. But I'm rambling.

Thank you. For all of it, Harry. For helping me bury the dog when he kicked it once too often. For you and Verlinda taking the new dog my mom gave me because she just couldn't believe Abner would do something like that and "surely, if he did, it was an accident and he won't do it again." My kids loved playing with Snow at your house. I thought the name was silly, until the day they were talking about loving to play with Snow and Abner thought they meant the kind that falls in the winter. That silly name helped us keep the secret dog a secret! Verlinda was so good with them. They still miss their Auntie Verlinda and her cornbread. They never thought mine was as good. Just proves they know their cornbread!

I know you love me, Harry, but I know you don't love me like you loved your Verlinda. You always lit up when that girl walked into a room. Even when she was so sick at the end, you never had eyes for anyone but her. But

Zane flipped the paper over, then looked in the envelope to see if he was missing something.

"There's no more. That's all she wrote. But it's enough. It makes sense now. Grandad always scared me. No one ever left me alone with him." Juliet laughed bitterly. "They had a 'wake' when he died. It always felt more like a celebration of his death than his life. I guess it was."

Zane gently brushed her bangs to the side. "Your Grammie was a strong woman, and you are just as strong as she was, Juliet."

Resting her head against his hand, Juliet released the tension it felt like she had been holding her whole life. "That's sweet, but she could do a lot of things I can't."

Zane pushed her back, holding her shoulders and looking her in the eye. "Don't you ever say that. You know how it would make her feel. I don't ever want to hear another word about how good she was at fixing things in the house, now that we know why she and your Aunt Marilyn are so good at it. Ripped out plumbing fixture? Hole in the wall? Water damage from an overflowing tub? Door off its hinges? The list of what they could fix puts a lot of handymen to shame. And now we know it's all the things your Grandad busted because Harry Lynch made sure he knew if he ever hurt his wife or kids that bad again, it would be repaid with interest.

"They fixed a lot of holes to get that good with plastering. I promise you, the only holes I put in our walls are because I'm accident-prone when I carry big things.

"Now," he took the letter, gently folding it and tucking it inside a nearby drawer, "I think it's time we let the past go and look toward the future." He gently put his hand on her stomach. "I don't know about you, but I am ready for the next phase in our life—dinner. I'm starving. We should try the special at the Gardens tonight."

"Sounds great! And I need to remember how happy Grammie and Harry were at the end. I remember the day she forgot who Abner was, but she never forgot Harry."

Dagnabit Belle

Chuck Thompson

Belle had been wanting, for a long time, to go north of the cabin to see what happened there. Her best friend, a Burmese-Hound mix named Barry, lived about two miles away in that direction. Ever since the big flash, she had not been able to catch any scent of him. The wind often carried Barry's smell, and other familiar ones, to her. But now the smells from that direction were all different. Ever since the flash and big boom happened. The humans got really scared and tense that day. It made her scared too. All the magic human things that made lights and sounds had gone silent for a long time. She heard more gunshots than usual since the flash. The air smelled different and the night sky was much darker than it used to be.

It wasn't just Barry that seemed to be missing. She couldn't smell the farms that were to the north. And nothing of the nice humans who lived up there. In particular, the Gonnegals had five children. They were full of hugs, giggles, kisses, and belly-rubs. And they loved to play chase and ball. Her own human, Robert Butcher, was pretty good at rubs and pets, but definitely not running and chasing, and not so much ball either. She understood. He was an old human and he just couldn't go like newer people. He did ride the thing with two wheels and that was a lot of fun. He could go fast when he was on it, and she loved chasing him down the roads. He also drove a big red truck and Belle thought she liked that even better than the two-wheel thing. Hanging her head out the window was so delicious. For some reason, rides in the truck were now rare. She missed them.

Robert had been sad ever since the flashy thing happened. She could tell from the tone of his voice, the way he held himself, and because he just had no excitement in the things he did. He used to whistle and hum. Not anymore. Belle thought it had something to do with the humans that used to come to the cabin almost every weekend but had not been back since the thing. Belle could tell from their smells that they were family to Robert and he was always happy to see them. But they seemed to be gone now and their scents had faded away. She also sensed that someone else, a female human, had lived in the cabin for a very long time. She was gone before Belle came to live with Robert as a puppy. The female's scent was small and faint now but it was everywhere inside the cabin, particularly in the kitchen and the room where Robert slept. Belle thought Robert missed her too.

For a while after the flashy thing Robert had been so strict about keeping her on the leash or in the cabin. She didn't understand this, because normally they went on a walk every day and she could zip back and forth in the woods and chase rabbits, squirrels, and lizards. They still did walks, but always on the leash.

Today, she could tell that Robert was restless. Most mornings, the first thing he did when he woke up was let her in his bedroom and then he would go back to bed and they would snuggle for a while. She would happily push up as close to him as she could. But today, he got up early, fed her, and then left out the back door. But the door hadn't clicked like it usually did.

She remembered that she could hook a claw under a thing on the bottom of the door to pull it open. Belle opened the door and sniffed around to see where Robert was. Nothing. He was probably at the barn down the hill, but she could hear no sounds of him. This was good. If he called her to come back, she would have to obey. Getting away unseen was the key. Robert might be mad when she got back and then her name would be Dagnabit-Belle. That's what her name was every time Robert was angry with her. She hated that name. But that's the worst that would happen. Some humans beat their dogs, but Robert never did. He wouldn't even stay cross very long. A little shoulder-sag and some sad-eye and not only was the angry gone, but she usually got a treat.

So, she was out. And headed north. Carefully at first, and then, when she figured she was far enough away, she started to sprint in Barry's direction. She couldn't wait to find him and play wrassle. Barry was so good at wrassle. He weighed as much as three of her but was just the right amount of rough and tumble and no bites. Afterwards, they could go find the creek and roll in the cool mud. For some reason, Robert didn't like her muddy and smelly. Humans were hard to figure. What was better than a good dirty stink?

Belle had been running for a while when she slowed and then stopped. The hair on her back stiffened and she tensed. Something ahead was wrong. It smelled sharp and spicy like nothing in her memory. It reminded her a little of the machines she sometimes got near when she and Robert went into Grantville. It also reminded her of the sharp scents that came off the long ropy things on the tall poles that seemed to follow all the roads. She crept closer and could see a strange wall. The sides were so smooth. Even smoother than the glass in the windows at the cabin. It wasn't right. Not at all. She was sure it had never been there before.

On the other side of the wall things were also not right. She should be able to sense Barry, the farms, and the humans by now. Instead, it was all woods, and rotting leaves, and she caught whiffs of some animals. Rich earthy smells, which could be good, but not if they weren't supposed to be there. And the animals were not the same kind she was used to. She knew every rabbit, squirrel, possum, and coon anywhere near the cabin. Some of these new ones were similar, but definitely different. They smelled...older and...rawer.

Belle stopped and whined a bit. She looked back in the cabin's direction. Eventually, she decided that Barry couldn't be that much farther. She would jump up the wall and get a good sniff. She was sure she could find him. Belle leapt. She had to grab the top and pull herself up. But at the top, she still couldn't find Barry—or any of the things that should be there. She decided to go a little bit farther and do some circles. Surely, she would pick up something familiar. On her second circle, she came across a creek that seemed familiar. There was a path on the other side and... just maybe...

No, the path wasn't anything she knew. Something deer-like had been using it, but no humans.

These woods were quieter than they should be. Belle perked her ears and pointed them everywhere. Yes. Too quiet.

It was then that Belle decided she needed to give this up and go home. For some reason, neither Barry nor the Gonnegals were where they were supposed to be. And all the farms and fields were gone. It was just woods. Woods not known to her. Her initial enthusiasm was all gone now, replaced by a steady creeping anxiety. She thought about it a while and realized she had left the cabin some hours ago. Time had flown by. Robert would not be happy and probably was looking for her. Belle cocked an ear to listen for his voice. Maybe he was calling her. Nothing. She decided she would start back.

After a short time, Belle realized she had made an awful mistake. A rising breeze, together with her circling, had confused the back trail. She was having trouble finding it. The strengthening wind was running south and moving the smells away from, rather than toward, Belle. Tracking back north, and then east and west to find her path helped, but each time she moved south, she lost it again. Eventually, she came back to the creek, but at a different point. A rain had started and before long, her back trail was so faint and diffuse that she could no longer tell which way to go. Anxiety climbed to fear and Belle whined and began barking. Maybe Robert would hear and come for her. She barked as loud and long as she could, but it didn't seem to work.

Just then, a fox screamed from somewhere nearby. She could tell it was a fox but it was unlike any fox she had ever heard before. It had a high, screeching voice and she didn't like it at all. Normally, they were not a danger, but they were still nothing to be trifled with. Males in heat, or mothers with young, could be vicious fighters. Belle was very sorry that she had ever opened the back door and run. This place could keep its screaming foxes and empty forest all to itself. If she could just get back to Robert, she would jump in his arms and cuddle in their favorite chair and not even mind if he called her Dagnabit and scolded her. She wouldn't even ask to go on walks, or to play ball, if she could just find him. She started to howl her sadness but cut it off when she remembered the fox nearby.

The light was fading from the sky about the time that Belle realized she was totally lost. She thought she caught wisps of her back trail from time to time but it was now so faint that she could not reason out its meaning, or the right direction to go. Fatigue and hunger filled her, and the forest was starting to come alive with night animals. Other than the fox, she had neither seen nor heard anything large, but the sounds she did hear were not comforting. She smelled animals she did not know. And she was in a place she had no memory of. Belle thought of doing some larger circles, hoping to find some clue to her whereabouts but was so exhausted that, when she came on a hole at the base of a big oak, she decided she better crawl in and get some sleep before trying again.

Belle slept fitfully that night. Noises and animal calls kept waking her. Once, a snuffling creature came close but her growls were enough to send it off.

She awoke to a misty and cold morning. Wisps of vapor floated over the ground and around the trees. Her breath clouded in front of her. Hunger roiled her stomach and Belle thought of Robert's warm lap and the kibble waiting at her cabin somewhere.

Home had to be south, and Belle had a shaky idea of the direction. Smell and sound were, by far, her best tools, but neither seemed to be much help right now. So, she took a guess and trotted off.

Perhaps an hour later, Belle found a spot where a rabbit had crossed her path. It was recent and must be nearby. Normally rabbits were pure entertainment, but she was so hungry that she couldn't think of anything but sinking her teeth into it and devouring the meat. Belle turned up the rabbit's trail, trotted for a while, and then slowed to a slow stalk as the scent became overpowering. It was near and upwind, which was perfect. Belle pushed through some ferns with barely a whisper and spotted the rabbit not a yard away. It was nibbling on a plant and unaware of her. But a finger of doubt poked her when she saw it. This rabbit was huge. Maybe half Belle's size. But a rabbit is a rabbit and a dog is a dog. Belle was not going to back away from any rabbit and that was for sure.

She took a few slow quiet steps and then leaped. Just as planned, she grabbed the rabbit's throat and bit down. She tried to shake the thing back and forth until there was a snap, but that didn't happen. The rabbit was so heavy that Belle couldn't manage to fling it. To her surprise, the rabbit twisted into her and gave her several sharp kicks to the stomach. Belle could feel its raking claws slice into her underbelly. No rabbit had ever fought her back. They all just quickly died. Belle yelped in pain and the rabbit broke free and ran into the brush. She started to give chase but her belly was on fire and she stopped and curled in to examine herself. A series of gashes were bleeding little rivers of blood and Belle found it difficult to get back up. Instead, she lay for a while and licked, trying to get the blood flow stopped.

Exhausted, Belle slept for a while where she lay. On waking, she could tell that half the day had passed. It hurt so much to get up, but she knew she had to. Fear now threatened to overwhelm her reasoning. She whined and started to walk stiffly downhill. So thirsty. She remembered down usually meant water and kept going. After an hour or so, Belle came on a creek. Different from yesterday's creek. It was smaller and cleaner. She lapped the water in until she couldn't take any more. The water seemed to help the hunger, at least for a little while. But it wasn't much longer before Belle's stomach began writhing again. She was sure she had never been so hungry before. Things seemed fuzzy and it was hard to think. Part of her wanted to just lay down and not get up. Not knowing any other way to go, Belle moved downslope with the stream.

It was getting late when she spotted a lighter area ahead. She quickened her pace and eventually pushed out of the woods, through the grass, and onto a road of sorts. But not any road in her memory. Belle looked up and down the road, sniffed, and listened hard. She thought, and then was sure, she heard clanking and clinking sounds approaching from the east. Moving to the shoulder of the path, Belle watched in the direction of the sound and, eventually, humans appeared. First heads, then bodies, and finally legs, as they crested a hill. They were dressed as no human she ever saw. They had thick coats and big boots and carried full packs on their backs or shoulders or hung from poles. Some had the largest hats she had ever seen, with long feathers sticking out. There was a whole pack of them. A sad and starved-looking horse pulled a cart. The humans definitely were tense. She could tell they were hungry and sad. She could smell blood on some of them, mainly from ones that had no boots or shoes of any kind. Human feet were not nearly as good as dog feet. They had to take special care of them. Humans like this meant danger.

As the first of the group approached, Belle crept up to them, belly dragging the ground in submission. She didn't get a good vibe from them at all but knew she needed help, and these were the only humans she had seen in two days. One of the men in front was about to pass her and she raised a paw and gave out a small whine. The man stopped, looked down at her, and frowned. Belle had made a mistake. Before she could scramble back, the man kicked out at her, catching her in the side. He muttered loud words that she could not understand but they were plainly ugly. The kick was enough to lift her partly in the air and fling her back to the shoulder of the road. Without looking back, the man moved on. No one in the group looked at her. She whined again, this time in pain. She tried to slink farther into the weeds.

Despite her torment, she smelled the dogs before she saw or heard them. A lot of dogs. And they smelled...wrong. Wild and rotten. The kind of dogs that had no person of their own. They were following at the back of the man-pack. Belle winced at the pain in her side and inched back away from the road hoping to find cover. Get out of sight. Some of the dogs passed by but a tan bitch with a curly tail stopped opposite Belle, sniffed the air, and launched into a heated alarm bark. The entire pack alerted and most of them rushed in her direction. It wasn't long before they were all snarling, barking, and surrounding her. They lunged in and nipped. Belle was no fighter, but they gave her little choice. She tried to snarl and bark back but also signaled her willingness to submit. It didn't seem to be working. One of the larger dogs waited until she turned to deal with one attack and he lunged in and grabbed her by the right hind and bit down hard. Another, smaller dog leaped at her neck. At that point, Belle was ready to give up.

"Nein! Nein! Böser Hund!"

The dogs backed off. A girl was swinging a stick back and forth and hitting the dogs attacking Belle. Some of them growled at the girl but a man joined her. He was armed with a much larger stick and cracked one of the bigger dogs in the head. It yelped and ran off. The rest seemed cowed by the big dog's retreat and followed him back into the road.

The girl knelt beside Belle and stroked her. Belle looked up at her and wagged her tail. The girl was talking to the man and Belle hoped they might help her. But the man shook his head and gently pulled the girl away. Before she left, the girl reached into her pocket and tossed a piece of bread down. The man frowned again but said nothing. Soon the people, the dogs, and the horse were gone out of sight and Belle was alone again.

Her leg was bleeding and her stomach wounds were open again. She was so tired. And hungry. Belle remembered the bread and pulled herself over and wolfed it down. Nothing had ever tasted so delicious. But there was so little of it. She tried to stand and found she could put no weight on her injured hind leg. She decided to get some rest and try again later. She drifted quickly into a troubled sleep.

Belle woke to the pre-dawn birds singing to each other. A light frost coated the grass and she shivered at the cold. She found that, though her pain had lessened some, the leg was very stiff and her wounds were thickly crusted with dried blood and bits of leaves. Belle pulled herself back up to the road and glanced both ways. She started a three-legged hop in what she hoped was the right direction. She would rest, then move some more, and rest again. As the day wore on, the rests got longer and the hopping in-between got shorter until, finally, she just lay down and let her head sink to the ground.

She dreamed. And in her dream, she was outside the cabin and Robert was calling her in for dinner. "Belle. Belle. Here Belle!" She could smell wood smoke from the chimney, and the mice that lived under the porch, and the old rug, and all the other wonderful things about home. It was a good dream.

"Belle. Belle. Here Belle! Here girl!" Why was Robert still calling? She was right there at the front door waiting to be let in. She reached out a paw in her dream. Her own movement stirred her from her sleep. Belle opened her eyes but hadn't the will to lift her head.

"Belle! Here Belle!" So, she was still dreaming. Although the call was a long way off now. It had been so clear and close in her dream. No, something told her. You are awake. The call came again, but more faintly. "Belle. Here Belle." It sounded like her Robert. Somewhere up ahead. Belle lifted herself up.

She fell. And tried again. This time she got up and started hopping in the direction of the call. She heard it again and, as she crested a rise in the road, she thought she saw a figure in the distance. He was riding a two-wheel thing. It had to be him. Belle barked as loud as she could and hobbled and hopped down the road. She fell twice but picked herself up again. Bark. Bark. But he didn't seem to hear and, worse still, he was moving away. NO. This just couldn't happen. Belle pulled everything she had left in her and flung herself down the road. It was really little more than a trot but she thought she would die with the effort. Her body screamed at her. And then he was gone, passing out of sight around a curve. Belle stopped and howled and barked in despair. She was spent and could do no more than stare at the spot she last saw him. Belle lay her head down again.

"Belle!" The dream again. This time, no voice argued with the dream. She was in Robert's lap, and he was stroking her. "Oh Belle...sweet girl...sweet girl." He gently grasped her head and leaned his cheek onto hers. Belle opened her eyes again and realized it wasn't a dream. She was in Robert's arms. He had turned around and found her. Even though it hurt to do so, Belle wagged every part of her body and turned her head to lick him—on the cheeks, his forehead, his brow, his eyes. She licked away the salty wetness streaming down his face. She heard him say, over and over, "Dagnabit Belle." But he said it in a new way. And she didn't mind at all.

The Grand Adventure
of Baron Munchhausen
in the
Land of the Americans
By Robert F. Lowell

The Grand Adventure Of Baron Münchhausen In The Land Of The Americans

Robert F. Lowell

Friends, you have never known me, Hilmar Ernst Freiherr von Münchhausen, to lie or exaggerate. Indeed, while certain vile, slanderous calumnies portray members of my noble family as prevaricators and fabulists, we von Münchhausens have always held ourselves to the highest standards of truthfulness and accuracy. Therefore I am sure you will give due credence to the story of how I personally saved the Americans of Grantville from the most fearsome, predacious beast ever to stalk the forests of the Germanies and received from them a magnificent gift.

I did not go to Grantville seeking fortune and glory. Indeed, I did not intend to go to Grantville at all. In September of 1633, attended by my man Peter, I journeyed to Thuringia-Franconia to ask the illustrious Wilhelm, Duke of Saxe-Weimar, for assistance in rebuilding my family's splendid Renaissance castle at Leitzkau. The same rapacious barbarians who sacked and burnt Magdeburg under Count Tilly—may he rot in Hell's Eighth

Circle—destroyed Leitzkau soon afterwards. My friends, the tears I wept when I saw the charred timbers and shattered stones of the castle where I spent many happy years of my childhood would fill a prince's christening cup. No less bitter were the tears of the common folk of the region who, deprived of work at the castle and its surrounding estates, faced the specters of penury and starvation. When I related the sad tale to His Imperial Majesty Gustav Adolf some months after the great victory at Alte Veste, he graciously granted me leave from my service with his light horsemen to secure what means I could to restore my ancestral home to its former glory.

My intention was not to implore Duke Wilhelm for aid on the strength of our familial connection, which I must admit is rather tenuous. I would instead approach him as a member of the Fruitful Society, the scholarly association dedicated to the preservation and enrichment of the High German Language, of which he was a founding elder. As concrete proof of membership in the Society I, like all my Fruitful fellows, wore a gold medallion bearing the Society's palm tree emblem.

That same medallion glinted in the autumn sun as Peter and I rode north along the old Prague road that fateful morning. In its reflection I swear I saw the face of my dear departed mother, who always considered me unworthy of the Society's august company, frowning on me from a stern saintly height. "Wastrel!" she scolded. "You think you can achieve what your sober older brother Liborius cannot and restore your precious little castle?" Mother rarely came to Leitzkau. "Ha! You disgrace the name of your valiant *landsknecht* grandfather! You think you can get whatever you want by flashing your father's blonde locks and sky-blue eyes, but your fool's errand will only come to grief! Listen to me, you—"

A fusillade of musketry drowned out Mother's voice. The unmistakable deep roar of arquebuses like the Imperials used at Breitenfeld echoed from beyond a bend in the road ahead. Sharper shots rang out moments later, singly and in rapid bursts.

Peter and I calmed our horses. Instinct and bitter experience told me it would be useless to formulate a plan without reconnaissance. Accordingly, I rode at a gallop to the base of the lightly wooded hill that hid the scene of battle, where I tied off my mount and proceeded on foot, silent as a starving cat at a fishmonger's. I kept low as more shots boomed and clouds of smoke obscured the sky, smelling like rotten eggs in the Devil's kitchen. When I attained the crest, I saw tarnished morions and dented breastplates gleaming among the trees on both sides of a blind curve. A perfect spot for an ambush. From my vantage point I could see thirteen soldiers, six armed with muskets. Their slow rate of fire and undisciplined volleys told me they were a band of deserters rather than an Imperial patrol. I peered through the smoke to see at whom they were shooting.

I saw a mechanical dragon.

Red in color with a metallic sheen, it approximated a bull elephant in length and girth, but not in stature, as it crouched with its head to the ground and hindquarters raised. Its wide-open mouth revealed rows of jet-black teeth and steam issued from a single nostril set between round yellow eyes. Horns great and small adorned the top of its head. Metal disks the size of wagon wheels, rimmed in black, lay to either side. I judged those to be shoes, thrown or shot off, from its forefeet. Its wings were folded straight back against its body, which was laden with crates and barrels, doubtless impeding its ability to fly. Two figures kneeled among the cargo, shouldering arms that looked like carbines but fired much faster than any wheellock could hope to. Two more brandished similar weapons from apertures in the creature's skull. The dragon's tail hung close to its body, like the flukes of a whale. I knew at once that such a machine, such weapons, and such people could only be American.

In other circumstances, the Americans would make short work of a ragtag mob of ruffians, but that morning the bandits clearly had them at a disadvantage. They were outnumbered, their damaged metal monster was immobile, and their intermittent and careful fire suggested they would run out of ammunition before long. The thought that barbarians like the ravagers of Magdeburg and Leitzkau would soon enjoy victory, murder, and plunder boiled my von Münchhausen blood. I could ride back to Saalfeld and raise the alarm, but by the time any help arrived the Americans would be done for. What would my renowned martial grandfather do in this situation?

Perhaps his spirit gave me the answer. An arquebus shot knocked a barrel off the dragon's back. It tumbled onto the road, raising a great cloud of dust. In that cloud I saw my plan of action. I crept back down the hill, galloped to meet my waiting manservant, handed him my greatcoat, and explained my plan. As he prepared for his part, I verified that my pair of eighteen-bore wheellock pistols were fully spanned in their saddle holsters. (Americans, I later learned, would size them at .637 caliber.) Satisfied that all was ready, I spurred my mount back to the bandits' position.

I rounded the bend in the road and made a great show of surprise at spotting the marauding deserters. I wheeled my horse toward one of the musketeers, drew and cocked my pistols, and fired them one after the other at the miscreant. From a hundred yards both struck home with fatal effect. Before any foe could return fire, I raced back around the bend and out of their sight.

At the sound of my pistols' twin reports, Peter zigzagged his gelding along the road, dragging our coats to raise mighty gouts of dust. He barked orders and shouted replies as if readying a patrol of dragoons to attack. On my return I did the same and blew my hunting horn to complete the illusion.

My ruse worked precisely as I planned. In moments, we heard the remaining bandits scatter like chickens before a fox and flee into the surrounding woods. Parting shots from American weapons hurried the cowards on their way. After assuring ourselves of their departure, Peter and I approached the Americans at a moderate pace so as not to be mistaken for more highwaymen. This and Peter's superb command of the English tongue ensured that we were well-received when we reached the stricken conveyance, which we learned was not a mechanical dragon but a *pickup truck*.

The truck's master, a young man named Zach Carroll, explained that one of his crew members was wounded in the thigh and that damage to their vehicle made it incapable of movement under its own power. We quickly agreed that sending Peter to Grantville to summon help was the best course of action. I would remain with the Americans in case the bandits rallied and resumed their attack. That possibility and the wounded man's condition caused us no little anxiety until, a few hours later, three vehicles like the stricken pickup arrived with a physician and ten heavily armed Americans. Still, the time we spent waiting for rescue was not unpleasant, particularly because one of the crew was a fetching young woman called Ella. I had not noticed her considerable charms from a distance because she wore the same indigo-dyed trousers favored by working American men and women. Hers were quite close-fitting, no doubt for riding, and suited her most admirably.

We were informed that it would not be safe to transport our horses in the trucks, so one was detailed to accompany Peter and our mounts while the rest of us rode the vehicles to Grantville. Sadly, I did not make the journey seated next to Ella, but beside a stout bearded man named Howard Carstairs who said he served in the Germanies with the American army and spoke some future version of my native tongue that I found challenging to understand. Though the seats and other interior appointments lacked ornamentation, they were more comfortable than the most luxurious coach. I would later come to understand that this was very much in keeping with the American character. They could work untold wonders, but eschewed ostentation in favor of practicality. In such style we arrived in the storied town of Grantville.

* * *

Friends, cataloging all the wonders I saw in my four days among the Americans would take many volumes. The town's overall appearance bespeaks peace and prosperity. It consists of one- or two-story houses sprawled among wide streets, lacking walls to pen in the populace or high towers to overawe them. I will limit myself here to two further observations.

It is often said that all Americans are fantastically wealthy and live in great luxury. This is not the case. Like all peoples, they have their rich, their poor, and their people of modest means. One often observes this range of circumstances within the same family, such as the McCarthys whose hospitality it was my privilege to enjoy during my time in Grantville. However, while the homes of the wealthy are spacious and well-constructed, they do not approach the size and grandeur of even the smaller country houses of European nobility like my beloved, war-ravaged Leitzkau Castle. Likewise, the poorest in Grantville have comfortable dwellings constructed of steel and boasting of clean water piped directly in and night soil and other foulness piped immediately out. These *trailers*, as they are called, would be the envy of any burgher in Germany. Moreover, like all homes in Grantville, they are furnished with devices that somehow, on the reverse side of curved glass screens, reproduce pictures moving with such realism and rapidity that they can depict the action of a play as it unfolds on a stage many miles away. I saw with my own eyes how rich and poor alike witness these performances in their own homes. This is but one example of how the true miracle of American wealth lies in the ordinary affluence of the common people.

One also hears that all American women are stunningly beautiful. This, I am happy to report, is absolutely true. The smile of every American girl glows like a full summer moon. Female faces are free of pock-marks and the town abounds with figures that would grace the canvases of Master Reubens. While some regard the immodest dress affected by Grantville women as an indication of corrupt morals, I consider it a sign of closeness to the Edenic ideal. I was quick to remark on the town's abundance of loveliness to my hosts, who credited it to good nutrition, pure mountain air, and the ministrations of surgeons who specialize in care of the teeth. After close and detailed observation, I would also credit their habit of daily bathing with scented soap, which, as well as having sanitary benefits, yields pleasant rewards both aesthetic and social. I understand that the Americans have founded a faculty of chemistry at the University of Jena. Making soap widely available at affordable prices would be a contribution to the health and happiness of mankind second only to Prometheus' theft of fire.

Health concerns, in fact, led to my confrontation with the great beast. At dinner one evening at the McCarthy home, a veritable feast which Lady McCarthy prepared in a remarkably short time without cooks or kitchen maids to assist her, Doctor James Nichols, a Moorish surgeon, lamented that a boy named Scott urgently required an operation.

"He's allergic to ether," Nichols explained, "and we're all out of other anesthetics. If I operate on him without pain killers, he's likely to die of shock."

"Perhaps you could use *chaga*," I suggested, with Peter acting as my interpreter.

"*Chaga*? What the heck is *chaga*?"

"It is a fungus that grows on birch trees, eventually killing them. It achieves full potency when the tree dies."

The healer furrowed his brow. "I've checked every book on medicinal plants I could get hold of, including Doctor Abrabanel's manuals, and none of them mentioned it."

"*Chaga* is not widely used in the civilized regions of Europe. I learned of it from His Imperial Majesty's Finnish cavalry. They employ it to ease the pain of wounds and occasionally for spiritual enlightenment."

"You mean they use it to get high," Nichols said. Upon translation I found that a most evocative expression for which the Fruitful Society must derive a German equivalent.

"Where can we find some?" the younger McCarthy asked.

"Anywhere there are birch trees," I said. "In mature form it resembles a fire-scar."

The surgeon nodded. "That funky Finnish fungus may be Scott's only hope."

Fueled by delectable morsels containing tiny bits of solid chocolate, a delicacy which until then I thought could only be savored as a drink, we planned a search of the woodlands near Grantville. Lady McCarthy periodically offered us more coffee, which I politely declined, as I found the American version of that Turkish beverage to have all the flavor and strength of burnt toast. We had only a few hours' sleep before our search parties mustered.

* * *

At first light, Doctor Nichols and I instructed dozens of assembled volunteers before they ventured into the forest in pickup trucks. Upon reaching their assigned dispersal points, our searchers paired off to seek for *chaga*. Each pair included one person with medical training and one experienced forager, hunter, or forester. All the Americans carried firearms, as is their custom. I was most fortunate to be partnered with Mistress Kristin Washaw, a capable young nursing student whose golden hair and chestnut eyes gave her the enticing look of a forest dryad. Neither of us spoke the other's language, so I patted my sword and pistols to reassure her of my readiness for any possible danger. Kristin inspected her own pistol, of the type that carried half a dozen charges in a revolving drum, to send me the same message

We sought for hours until Kristin spied a birch richly adorned with dry leaves, betokening its recent demise. Inspection soon revealed a huge mass like the coals of a long-extinguished fire clinging to its bark. Its scaly texture and almost imperceptible odor of freshly tilled earth confirmed it as *chaga* in the prime of potency. The young nurse carefully cut the fungus free while I stood guard nearby, watching the forest and observing her technique.

A scream louder than a thousand harpies shredded the calm of the autumn forest. In a single motion I drew a pistol and spun on my heels to see a lioness leap from the underbrush. I swear on my mother's soul that the creature was as long as a bull and as broad as a Lipizzaner stallion, lacking a mane but covered nose to tail in tawny fur, with claws like tenterhooks and teeth like ivory daggers. Mad-eyed, it hurled itself straight toward its intended prey, the young nurse.

I fired my pistol at the monster, but my shot struck only the dead birch. At the same moment, Kristin stepped backwards and attempted to draw her weapon but slipped on dead leaves, struck her head on the roots of a gnarled oak, and fell unconscious to the forest floor. That misstep likely saved her life. The lioness sailed over her, tearing her padded jacket with its rear claws. Downy feathers flew, but no blood flowed. As I drew my second pistol, the creature wheeled about and crouched behind her fallen form. Licking its chops, it gazed at me like a tabby stalking a pigeon.

In that moment, friends, I was caught in the Devil's own dilemma. My shot would doubtless bring help in time, but at any moment the gigantic feline's jaws or claws could tear into my young companion. Even for an accomplished marksman such as myself, firing a second shot would run too great a risk of hitting Kristin. To get a clean shot I had to draw the creature out from cover. But how?

As the lioness held me with her golden eyes, I could see the face of an even more fearsome female. "Hilmar Ernst, you vain little fool," I heard Mother say. "You fancy yourself the mighty hero, flashing your sword, waving your pistols, flaunting your gold medal. Ha! What good will any of them do you now? Your quest for glory will cost this young lady's life. Pray that the creature kills you as well, so you won't have to carry the guilt for the rest of your worthless life!"

The beast's low growling banished the apparition, but Mother's words still tore at me. My weapons were indeed useless so long as the lioness held her position. I stood frozen in indecision. A shaft of autumn sun broke through the trees and glinted in the great cat's eyes. Still it waited, daring me to hopeless fight or fruitless flight, toying with me.

A desperate notion struck me like a leap into the snow after a Finnish sauna. Toys! For all its monstrous size, the creature was still a cat. With great care I reached into my shirt and drew out my gold Fruitful Society medal. I held it at arm's length and dangled it in the sun. The gleaming metal caught the light as it swayed. The lioness followed it with her eyes. All else stood still save for my pounding heart.

She pounced. I fired. We both hit our targets. She, thank God, leapt for my medal rather than my throat. Her jaws tore it from my grasp, leaving my hand still attached. I believe my bullet struck her in the shoulder, but

I could not be certain, as she bounded into the forest like a house cat with a mouse. I drew my sword in case she should resume her attack, but after a few moments I could neither see nor hear any trace of the golden-furred monster.

When I was confident she would not soon return, I sheathed my blade and ran to tend to Kristin, holding her head steady in my hands to prevent further injury until more Americans arrived to bear her safely back to Grantville.

* * *

Kristin was not seriously injured, thanks be to God. Thanks to Him, the surgical skills of Doctor Nichols, and the pain-relieving *chaga*, the operation on young Scott was entirely successful and a swift recovery was expected. Over the next few days, the feline monster occasioned some debate. Hunters failed to find the creature either dead or alive, prompting some skeptics to contend the great cat could not have been an American mountain lion—as no such beasts had been seen in this vicinity for over a century before the Ring of Fire—but rather only a lynx, common in the Thuringer Woods and indeed throughout Europe. Others argued that the paw prints it left behind were larger than any ever made by a lynx or its American cousin the *bob-cat*, lending support to my insistence that the predator I saw was of leonine size at the very least. All could agree, however, that many things unseen by human eyes dwell in the deep forest.

I rejoiced that I was able to play some small part in restoring young Scott back to health. My American hosts, and indeed all the people of Grantville, voiced their gratitude at every opportunity. I must confess, however, that my joy was tempered by the impending collapse of my plans to restore Leitzkau Castle. Duke Wilhelm owed my family no favors and the loss of my Fruitful Society medallion in circumstances to which only I could testify would dispose him unfavorably towards my case. I had driven off a man-eating lioness but could not banish visions of my childhood home fallen to eternal ruin. So low was my state, I found myself agreeing with Mother. I believed myself the most pathetic fool in the Germanies.

I lamented this prospect to my hosts during my final supper in Grantville. The very same company as that around the elder McCarthys' table the evening before the *chaga* hunt extended their sympathies. Endeavoring to cheer us, Lady McCarthy served sweetmeats she said once graced every American table but were now rare delicacies: *peanut butter cookies*. Her American guests reacted as if they had been served ambrosias of the gods, and indeed the honeyed aroma and earthy savor of those delectables evoked all the riches of Hades and Persephone. My hosts explained that their principal ingredient, nuts which grew beneath the ground rather than on trees, could only be obtained from the New World or occasionally from Spain. As they relished these morsels, my companions related treasured childhood memories involving other dishes made with the creamy delight. Their bittersweet tales struck chords of sympathy within me, and I remarked that their peanut butter was my Leitzkau, a happy part of their heritage they had hoped to pass on to their descendants but might now be lost to them forever.

The next morning, the day of our departure, I was awakened by thunderous rumbling and tremors reverberating throughout the McCarthy house. I feared an earthquake of biblical scale had struck Grantville until the vibrations calmed and Peter passed on my hosts' urgent invitation to join them on their front lawn.

Hastily making myself presentable I hurried out the front door half expecting to view a scene of devastation. Instead, I marveled at a mechanical menagerie arrayed on the adjacent residential avenue: drayage vehicles several times the size of McCarthy's pickup trucks; battering rams rolling on continuous metal carpets; elephantine contraptions with great buckets for snouts and multi-jointed mechanical arms for tails. I soon learned the latter two were called *bull-dozers* and *back-hoes*, but to me they were all earth-rending, smoke-belching monsters.

"Why—why have they come here?" I stammered.

"Because they want to help," old McCarthy answered.

My face radiated complete incomprehension.

"These are construction vehicles, earth movers, on their way to a job here in Grantville," McCarthy continued. "We can't spare the building materials you'll need for your castle, and we're in no position to lend you enough money, but once you get your hands on some, our heavy equipment and skilled workers can get the job done in record time. It's Grantville's way of saying thanks."

Friends, for the first and only time in my life, I was at a loss for words. With American workers and machines committed to the project, Duke Wilhelm could hardly refuse to support the rebirth of Leitzkau Castle. The finest architects from Vienna, Paris, even Constantinople, would duel with one another to direct the enterprise. The castle would become more beautiful on its gently sloped hilltop than it was in my golden-hued memories.

When I recovered the power of speech, I offered profuse thanks to my hosts and the town's other leading citizens. With my spirits fully restored, I tarried a few hours in the company of a most gracious lady before departing Grantville with deep joy in my heart. Americans are a people to whom much has been given, but from whom much more can be expected, and I assure you, friends, that is no exaggeration.

Adieu Anvers

Marc Tyrrell

Adieu Anvers

Adieu Anvers, adieu la noble ville.

Contraint je suis, de toi me separer

non pour mal faict, et non pour chose vile,

mais las pour une'a qui point comparer

on ne devroit Venus ni Helaine,

tant est la grace, qui gist en elle

dont le partir me fera doulce paine,

estant accompaigne d'une chose tant belle.

Adieu Anvers, adieu Anvers.

Farewell Antwerp, farewell noble city.

I am compelled to part from you,

not for wrongdoing, and not for vile things,

but for one to whom one should not compare

Venus nor Helen,

such is the grace that lies within her

whose departure will bring me sweet pain,

being accompanied by such a beautiful thing.

Farewell Antwerp, farewell Antwerp.

Noë Faignient, 1568

Laurids Huis, Antwerp
Thursday, April 15, 1632, 4:35 p.m.

Désirée looked up from her book, the 1580 edition of Plotinus published in Basel, when she heard the knock on her door. "Enter," she called out, marking her place with a strip of ribbon.

Samuel Laurids, banker and master of the house, stepped in, holding several letters. He closed the door behind him as she rose from her seat, giving him a curtsy. "Oh, sit down, Désirée," he smiled and took a seat opposite her. "Several messages came in for you, and I wanted to talk with you about them." He handed the letters to her. "Might I suggest you read the one from the *Veedor General* first? He sent me a note, so I already know what it says."

Désirée gave him a short smile, opened the sealed letter, and scanned it quickly, focusing on its core message.

It is most unfortunate that some at Court have become aware of your connection to last summer's investigation, and are starting to ask pointed questions that I have no desire to answer. Those who need to know of your involvement have known since last July and, upon consultation with them, they have suggested that it might be best if you were to leave Flanders. Knowing your circumstances, they are prepared to offer you the sum of two hundred and fifty guilders to facilitate that move.

Désirée, you took vile wounds in my service and it pains me to ask you to follow their suggestion, but I must ask it. These questions at Court must stop, and interest in last summer's investigation must subside, lest it imperil my entire mission here. Should you agree to leave, I will match the offered sum so that you will have five hundred guilders to establish yourself wherever you wish.

Désirée closed her eyes. *"Vile wounds"? Yes, I suppose having half the skin flayed off my back while being raped would count as "vile"!* It had taken nearly six months before her skin had healed enough to bear the touch of cloth, and another two months before she could walk without constant fear that she would tear the new skin open again. Even today, some nine months afterwards, she had to walk carefully and limit her lifting.

She opened her eyes slowly and looked at Samuel. "And what would you suggest, *Meester* Laurids?"

She saw Samuel lean back, watching her carefully. "I believe that Don Luis has an unfortunately good point. It..." Here he paused as if searching for the right words. "It seems to me that there is nowhere in Flanders you can go that will allow you to escape your past while, at the same time, allowing the interest at court to die down. And, were it to be generally known that the inspector general of the Army of Flanders was reliant upon you to solve the situation last summer, well, his position, or at least his standing, would be badly compromised."

Désirée let out a snort. Her past, as it were, consisted of being the only surviving child of a couple attainted for heresy and executed, followed by eight years as a whore. A high-class whore, but a whore just the same. *He's right. That will follow me anywhere in Flanders or Holland. Probably as far as the Catholic Rhine, now that I think about it.* "And do you have any suggestions, *Meester* Laurids?"

"Perhaps. But, please, read this other letter first."

She recognized the writing, and started to smile. "Alphons is *so* predictable," she said with a chuckle. "A letter every month enquiring after my health and fortune, and describing his experiences in that strange town from the future." She opened the letter and scanned it quickly, chuckling at some passages, until her eye caught on one paragraph.

I am most pleased to hear that you are, once again, able to walk. If, at some point, you would care to visit here, I would be most happy to guest you in any capacity that you desire. This is an amazing place in so many ways, and I believe that you would enjoy any time you spent here, as I would enjoy seeing you again.

Désirée raised an eyebrow, then shook her head, before looking at Samuel. "He says that he wants to guest me in Grantville."

Samuel chuckled, and she saw a wry grin appear on his face. "I suspected as much." He leaned back and sighed. "I'm afraid that Don Alphons Quixote is riding again." He shook his head, then looked her in the eyes. "He hasn't acted like this in well over a decade. I do believe," he said, steepling his fingers, "that he is smitten with you."

Désirée rolled her eyes and snorted. "At most, he is enamored of an illusion. He doesn't know me at all."

Samuel nodded. "That's as may be, but it does sound as if he would like to know you better. And," he flicked a finger towards the letter from Don Luis, "guesting with him may be the solution to your problem. At least," he shrugged, hands wide, "it will give you a safe space while you decide what you want to do."

Désirée cocked her head to the side. "Are you suggesting that I accept his offer?"

Samuel smiled gently. "Actually, I am." He shrugged. "It is a possibility I have been considering for some time. I have other contacts in Grantville and, from what I hear, it may be the best place for you to go, for now at any rate. Allow me to enumerate. Primus," he held up a finger, "they have no established religion, so the fate of your parents and brother will only evoke sympathy."

A second finger followed. "Secundus, they have an organization that is becoming both popular and influential—it is called the Committees of Correspondence—that was started by an ex-camp follower and prostitutes in Jena, so your former occupation may attract less stigma. Tertius,"—a third finger—"five hundred guilders may sound like a lot of money, but it isn't. Grantville, however, appears to have some excellent investment opportunities that would allow you to increase that amount."

The fingers dropped. "The final point I would make is that one of my contacts there, Maria Bergmannin, has informed me that she would be happy to help you get settled. She is," the smile left his face, "a force to be reckoned with, and I trust her judgment." Slowly, the smile grew again. "Let me also note that Maria knows Alphons, apparently fairly well, and he is, hmm, leery of opposing her, so, if he were to, ah, act in an untoward manner, you would have support."

Désirée snorted, then thought about his points. "Well, it might be the best solution. Certainly it's the obvious one on offer. Now I just have to figure out how to get there." She started to smile, somewhat ruefully. "And decide how to deal with Alphons."

Samuel chuckled. "The first I can help with. You should take Rachel with you as a chaperone and companion." Samuel's nineteen-year-old niece, Rachel, had helped nurse Désirée back to what health she now had. Rachel also compounded, and applied, the lotions that helped keep Désirée's new-grown skin supple. "The second?" He shook his head. "That is entirely up to you."

Leaving Antwerp
May 3, 1632, 6:15 a.m.

Getting to Grantville had, in the end, proven to be simple. Désirée and Rachel had joined a convoy of freight wagons delivering goods from Antwerp to Grantville for Alphons, riding in a specially built, light wagon. As they left Antwerp, Désirée glanced behind her at the receding walls, smiled, and started to sing.

Adieu Anvers, adieu la noble ville.

Rachel joined in on the alto, followed by three teamsters on different parts.

Contrait je suis, de toi me separer...

They continued singing as the walls slowly faded into the early morning mist.

Verbannen House, 300 Adams Street, Grantville
Tuesday, May 25, 1632, 5:22 p.m.

"I'm home, Hans," Alphons called out as he stepped through the front door.

"Oh, good! There's a courier packet from your father," Hans Baumgartner, his factotum, said as he handed a rather large packet of papers to Alphons.

"Thanks. And dinner is in...?"

Hans chuckled. "About an hour. You've time to go through the packet before then. I'll just bring you a glass of wine."

* * *

Alphons read the last page of the letter, feeling giddy. He threw it down on the desk and suppressed the urge to jump up and down in glee, settling for a single "Yes!", pumping his arm in the air.

Hans stuck his head around the corner. "What's got you acting like an unruly apprentice, Alphons?"

"She's coming, Hans," he said with what an American would call a shit-eating grin. "We need to get the guest room ready for two." Hans just rolled his eyes and nodded.

* * *

As he lay in bed that night, Alphons couldn't stop grinning. He knew his reaction was fanciful, but he couldn't help himself as a childish chorus of *Yes, she's coming!* blended with increasingly graphic images. In the back of his mind, the part that made him such a successful merchant and investigator, he heard a sigh. Always, when that part of his mind spoke, it was with the voice of one of his early tutors. *If you want to win this woman,* the voice said, *then you must strive to help her free herself. Do not command or demand, merely offer aid and support for* her *desires until she knows what they are.*

What? That makes no sense! The chorus in his mind yelled back, displaying even more fevered images. Alphons could feel the phantom pain of a cuff to his head. *Fool boy! She is not a cargo of wine or dyes! She is a living person who has been under the control of others! For the first time in her life, she is free of control. But she doesn't know who she is without those chains. Do* NOT *propose to put her in new ones! She will not thank you for it.* Alphons grimaced at the conflicting voices in his head, rolled over, and tried again to sleep.

Thuringen Gardens, Grantville
Thursday, June 3, 1632, 2:55 p.m.

Anna, Alphons' favorite waitress, walked over to him and said, "Jamie has a call for you, Alphons."

"Thank you, Anna." Alphons got up and went over to the bar. Jamie wordlessly handed him the phone.

"Thanks, Jamie." He took the phone. "Alphons Verbannen speaking."

"Hello, Alphons, it's Maria Bergmannin. I just heard from the border station that your convoy is here. You've got about an hour before they arrive at your house, so finish up your business and get home as soon as possible. I will be picking up Désirée and Rachel tomorrow morning at nine." She hung up before Alphons could say anything. Gobsmacked, he handed the phone back to Jamie, settled his bill, and dashed for the door.

Buffalo Street, Grantville
4:35 p.m.

The trip had taken Désirée and Rachel thirty-one days. New freight wagons were added as they went along until, by the time they arrived at the Ring of Fire, there were eighteen heavy wagons accompanying them, carrying a variety of goods destined for Alphons' warehouse in Saalfeld. The cattle, goats, and sheep had already left the convoy, headed for a slaughter yard.

Their wagon left the convoy at Marshall Street, turning left, while the rest moved onward toward Route 250. *Strange houses,* Désirée thought as they turned down the street, driving several blocks before turning left again on Adams Street, and then a hard right into a laneway. She spotted

Alphons coming down the stairs. Putting on her professional face, she sighed. "I do believe we are here, Rachel."

Once the wagon had stopped, she threaded her way to the back and descended, following Rachel. Coming around the back corner, she watched Alphons walking toward her, a silly smile on his face. "Désirée, I am *so* glad you decided to accept my invitation!"

Giving him a wary smile, she said, "Alphons, it is wonderful to see you again, my *friend*." The emphasis was slight but, to an astute observer, noticeable. Alphons' smile shifted; less silly and more professional. *Good*, she thought, *he got the message*.

Alphons' eyes flicked to the side. "Ah, Rachel. Samuel said you were coming. Let me introduce the two of you to my staff, and we can get you settled in." He gave them a wave, and led them over to a man and woman in their early forties, flanked by two boys and a girl. "Désirée, Rachel, may I present Hans Baumgartner and his wife, Elsa Meyerin?" He waited until Désirée nodded. "They used to run an inn which, unfortunately, disappeared in the recent unpleasantness."

Alphons smiled cryptically. "And these are their children, Johannes,"—a finger pointed at the older boy, maybe fourteen—"Heinrich,"—a second finger aimed at a twelve-year-old—"and Greta"—who appeared to be about ten. "They are all in school now, but do help around the place."

"Hans, Elsa, this is my good friend Désirée d'Anvers and her companion, Rachel Laurids, from Antwerp. Elsa, could you show Désirée and Rachel to their bedroom, while we get their luggage unloaded?"

D'Anvers? Désirée thought. *Well, somewhat accurate and better than nothing. I suppose I can live with it for now.*

* * *

Désirée deftly speared the last piece of venison on her plate, added a mushroom and sauce, and popped it into her mouth. *This is the best meal*

I have had since leaving Antwerp! She carefully mixed the egg noodles with the remaining sauce, then cut into the last of the squash and ate it.

Elsa was smiling at her. A novelty, that. She had never before seen servants who sat down with their betters for dinner, but Alphons seemed to encourage it. He even had all three of the children eating with them. "Like the squash?" Elsa asked with a smile.

Désirée nodded. "It's wonderful! It goes perfectly with the sauce. I've never tasted anything like it before."

Elsa laughed. "I got the recipe from one of Alphons' clients, a Master Cook from Italy. Well," her eyes flicked towards Alphons, "and his employer."

Alphons glanced up. "Sandy?"

Elsa nodded. "Yes. Sandy gave me the recipe for the venison and sauce, while *Maestro* Amendola gave me the squash recipe."

Désirée asked, "Is this San-dy a local noble or patrician?"

Both Alphons and Elsa started to laugh. "Sandy," Alphons said, "is a twelve-year-old boy who, along with his stepmother and a master blacksmith, has just started a company making kitchenware. He's a good cook in the up-time style, and he recently hired *Maestro* Amendola, a Master Cook from Milan, to help him learn modern cooking."

Désirée was shaking her head in bewilderment. "Wait. A twelve-year-old boy? How is that possible?"

Alphons just smiled. "Welcome to Grantville."

Verbannen House
Friday, June 4, 1632, 8:55 a.m.

Désirée and Rachel were waiting in Alphons' front parlor for Frau Bergmannin to arrive. *It really is a lovely room*, Désirée thought, as she looked around. The large windows looking out onto the street and the bookcases opposite them framed the room nicely. The furniture was all from the up-time: a large table—Alphons called it a desk—with a single chair in the window, several couches and chairs, and a few low tables. A large television on a low cabinet dominated the wall opposite the windows between the bookcases.

Alphons had brought everyone into the room the night before, and turned the television on to watch a movie—something called *The Wizard of Oz. I still can't believe that the Church hasn't sent the Inquisition after them!* Good *witches? Flying monkeys?* After seeing that, Désirée found the idea of a twelve-year-old running a company less surreal, if still bewildering.

She glimpsed a movement out of the corner of her eye, but it was gone before she could focus on it. A second later, a chime sounded and Hans opened the door. "Frau Bergmannin! Wonderful to see you again," she heard him say. "Come in, please."

Désirée could see an older woman walking in, maybe five foot six, with grey in her neatly pinned blond hair. "I take it that Alphons is out and about, Hans?"

Hans laughed. "Yes, he headed off to the warehouse right after breakfast. He did say he would be at his usual table at the Gardens by eleven if you, and the ladies, would care to join him for lunch. But, let me make introductions." Hans waved Maria into the parlor, and Désirée got her first good look. *Hmm, probably in her fifties, very fit. Piercing blue eyes set in a strong, rather than beautiful, face. I think I agree with Samuel; not a woman to cross.*

Désirée and Rachel rose as Hans entered. "Frau Bergmannin, these are Désirée d'Anvers and her companion, Rachel Laurids. Désirée, Rachel, this is Frau Maria Bergmannin."

Maria strode forward, hand outstretched. "Désirée, I am glad to meet you. Samuel has told me some of your story, and I have looked forward to making your acquaintance." She snorted, "Of course Alphons has been noticeably reticent, and tended to blush and change the topic whenever I brought you up." Maria cocked her head to the side, with a slight smile as her eyes took in Désirée. "I can see why," she said as her smile widened. "We must have a long chat, and find new ways to embarrass Alphons. He takes himself too seriously."

Désirée laughed. "Oh, yes! It will do him good."

Désirée was smiling as Maria turned to Rachel, whom she swept into a hug. "Rachel, I feel like I've known you all your life, even if we have never met. Samuel has been sending me stories about you forever, so meeting you in person is an absolute treat! And I want the *real* story behind Samuel's cryptic references to a teaching sister, a pony, and a stablehand."

Rachel burst out laughing. "Oh my, surely he didn't pass that on!"

"Only little bits."

Rachel smiled and wiped her eyes. "Um, well, maybe. But *not* in a public place!"

Maria was laughing. "That can be arranged," she said. "But, ladies, in the meantime, we have places to go and things to do. Do you have everything you need?" At their nods, she continued. "Right then, let's away."

Thuringen Gardens
11:48 a.m.

The most impressive thing about this morning was how ordinary it was, as if a whore opening an investment account was normal! Désirée thought, as she and Rachel followed Maria into the Gardens. *No! Stop that! You're not a whore anymore!* some part of her mind said, as she walked through the door. *Then what am I?* She had been asking herself that question since she left Antwerp, but still had no answer.

As she wended her way to the table where Alphons was sitting, she wondered if she would get any answers this afternoon after her so-called "placement tests". She snorted softly and, smiling ruefully, thought, *Maybe I'll go back to school.*

Alphons looked up from the notes he was making, then, smiling, rose to greet them. "Ladies, I hope you had a good morning?" He waved toward the other chairs at his table. "Please, sit. Anna should..." He glanced to the side. "Let me rephrase: Anna *is* here."

Anna rolled her eyes, and handed menus to Maria, Rachel, and Désirée. "Of course I'm here, Alphons. Ladies, I'm certain that Frau Bergmannin can answer any questions you may have about the menus, while I get you drinks. Frau Bergmannin? Small beer?" Receiving a nod, she looked at the others. "Ladies?"

Désirée smiled at Anna. "Maybe a glass of red wine?"

Anna nodded. "We have several reds. Alphons can probably give you a good idea of each, since we buy a lot of it from him."

Alphons nodded. "Sweet? Dry? Nutty?"

Désirée thought about that. "Maybe somewhat sweet, but with a full body."

Alphons flipped his eyes upwards, then down and smiled. "Rachel, are you interested in wine as well?" She nodded, and he continued, "Then I have the perfect selection. Anna, could we have a bottle of *Davids Blut*, please? And another glass of the Franconian, chilled. That should give everyone time to decide on food."

Anna nodded, then paused. "Oh, I should mention that anything on the menu with a six-pointed star beside its name is kosher. Just in case anyone is interested." That said, she headed off to get the drinks.

Rachel looked up in surprise. "They have a kosher kitchen?"

Alphons nodded. "It's small, just off the main kitchen. But there are more than enough Jews in town to make it worthwhile. Besides that," he shrugged, "some up-time food can be kosher. There's a thing called a 'smoked meat sandwich' that a lot of people like."

Rachel frowned. "What is a, uh, 'sand-witch'? Doesn't the Church object?"

Alphons laughed. "It's a 'sandwich', not 'sand-witch'. Named after some up-timer. It's pretty much anything served between two, or three, slices of bread." He smiled. "And no, the Church doesn't object. Well, at least not here in Grantville." He gave a slight shrug. "And if they object elsewhere? Well, I don't think anyone here would care. If they sent Inquisitors here, those Inquisitors would end up in jail."

Désirée was shocked. "Wait. What?"

Maria turned to her. "The Inquisition has no power, and no jurisdiction, here. The Americans have seen to that. If the Inquisition tried to come here and act as they normally do, they would be arrested. Or," she shrugged, "maybe just killed. It's one of the things I like about Grantville."

Désirée was struggling with that. *"The Inquisition keeps the faith pure!"* vied with *"Those bastards killed my family!"* "I, uh, find that hard to believe." She shook her head, trying to clear it. "I thought the Church operated here?"

"They do," Maria said while nodding. "They just don't operate as freely, shall we say, as they do elsewhere. Now," she rubbed her hands together as Anna returned and started distributing their drinks, "what's the special today, Anna?"

Verbannen House
4:25 p.m.

Désirée and Rachel were sitting in the front room dissecting the results of their placement tests. "I still find it amazing how well you did on that science test, Désirée." Rachel shook her head in wonder.

Désirée let out a small chuckle. "The Sisters who had the keeping of my childhood trained me well and, after that," she shrugged, "well, men like to talk about their interests, and some of them prefer a person who can ask intelligent questions." She chortled, "It gives them an opportunity to show off their knowledge." She settled back and shrugged again. "And if they are just bragging and don't really know much, well, that tells me a lot about their character. But you," she said, "did *much* better than I did in mathematics!"

Rachel blushed. "Well, it's one of those family things. The women in our family are expected to be able to calculate anything from shipping costs to profit margins to food requirements, as well as keep the books and run a household. I've had a *lot* of practice over the past few years and," she shrugged, "I've always liked mathematics. Anyway," she shrugged, "my uncle has charged me to look into investment opportunities here, given how well Alphons speaks of them."

Désirée gave a short laugh. "Maybe I should have you tutor me," she said with a smile. "So, we are both enrolled in up-time English, basic mathematics, and basic sciences. From what I understand, those last two are just to get us familiar with the symbols and terminology the up-timers use, before going much further."

Rachel was nodding. "Yes, that's my understanding as well. I'm pretty sure they will also go into some of the philosophy behind both their mathematics and sciences as well." She looked thoughtful. "I suspect that we will be finished with them, and placed in different courses, in the fall." Rachel looked Désirée in the eyes. "Do you know what you want to do here?" She waved her hand to encompass Grantville.

Désirée shook her head. "No, not yet. Only that I don't want to live on Alphons' charity forever."

Verbannen House
Tuesday, June 8, 1632, 7:05 a.m.

"Désirée, are you and Rachel free for dinner tonight?" Alphons asked as they walked into the dining room.

Désirée glanced at Rachel, who shrugged, before turning back to Alphons. "We could be. Is this something special?"

Alphons waggled his hand back and forth. "Maybe. I got a telephone call last night, after you two had gone to bed, asking me if I'd come over tonight to add some weight to a scheme Sandy's stepmother, Summer, is attempting. I hope she meant *gravitas* and not," slapping his belly, "actual weight! I do try," he said, a forlorn look emerging on his face, "to stay in shape."

Désirée stifled a laugh. Alphons would never be considered "slight" or "thin", but most of his weight was muscle, with just enough fat to shout "prosperous." "And you succeed, Alphons, with just enough extra *gravitas* to play the role of an affable merchant," she said with a smile.

Ooops! Best walk back on some of that or he'll get the wrong idea, Désirée thought, as she saw Alphons' pleased smile. Taking the smile off her face, she said "Maybe she wants you to beat up or kill someone? Or, maybe, just threaten them?"

Alphons winced. "Ah, I believe the scheme involves one of Sandy's school teachers. She probably just wants a successful merchant there, who has dealt with the business." Steadying himself, he said, "So, shall I pick the two of you up at the school? It's only a fifteen-minute walk from there to the Workshop." Receiving nods, he smiled.

Summer's Kitchen Workshop
5:52 p.m.

Alphons was waiting for them at 5:30 when their classes let out, holding a cloth bag with several straw-wrapped bottles. "For tonight," he said, by way of explanation, as he led them over to the Workshop. As they approached, Désirée couldn't help but be impressed by its size.

Alphons gave them a quick tour, starting on the ground floor, which contained a small foundry, multiple forges, and a kiln of a most unusual design, which piqued Désirée's interest. "I don't think I've ever seen a kiln like that," she said, wondering why it didn't go up the slope like ordinary kilns.

"It's an up-time design, I'm told. *Much* more fuel-efficient than our kilns," Alphons said. "And, if you look closely, they're using an old Roman technique, funneling all the heat up to the next floor, then the floors above that and, finally, out the roof. Come winter, they should be warm enough."

Désirée found herself nodding as they walked up a flight of stairs to the second floor. "This," Alphons said, gesturing to the entire floor, "is where they shape their pottery, assemble their mechanisms, and do their wood-working." Désirée looked around, seeing a number of heavy work-benches, many covered in incomprehensible pieces of wood, metal, and clay.

Alphons waited for Désirée and Rachel to nod, then led them up another set of stairs. "This is the heart of the Workshop: the kitchen. There are sleeping rooms for apprentices and journeymen on this floor as well. The floor above is for the masters. Ah," he said as a man of about thirty looked up, "Giovanni!" Alphons called out in Italian. "Are you free?"

"A minute, Alphons." He turned and said something to the youngster next to him, then nodded and walked towards them, smiling. Désirée examined him as he approached. Tall, maybe five foot eight by the up-time measure. Shoulder-length wavy black hair tied back, and a striking, angular face with dark, piercing, eyes. *Extremely well-muscled arms and shoulders,* she thought.

And, Désirée noted, *he moves like a dancer; must be all that time spent dodging others in a busy kitchen,* she thought as he deftly twisted out of the way of a young boy, maybe six, carrying a tray outside.

"Alphons!" Giovanni cried. "So wonderful to see you, my friend. But please, tell me who these visions of delight are!"

Désirée smiled, while Rachel blushed. *Yes, Italian,* Désirée thought, as Alphons shook his head. "Giovanni, Giovanni. What am I going to do with you?"

"Introduce me to your lovely companions, of course!"

Alphons chuckled. "Of course. Désirée, Rachel, allow me to present *Maestro* Giovanni Amendola, a master cook from Amalfi, via Rome and Milan." Giovanni bowed elaborately, causing Désirée's smile to increase, and Rachel's blush to deepen. "Giovanni, this is my good friend Désirée d'Anvers, and her companion Rachel Laurids, from Antwerp." They both curtsied.

Alphons held out the bag he was carrying. "For tonight's festivities."

Giovanni took it, then slapped his head. "Ahh! I am remiss!" Désirée's smile widened at the theatrics. "You *must* have wine! I already have some of the Franconian *piscio di cavallo* that Alphons likes chilling, but what would you ladies like?"

Alphons flicked a finger at the bag. "Maybe some of the *Davids Blut*, Désirée, Rachel?"

Désirée nodded, "That would be pleasant. I developed a taste for it over the past year."

"Bide but a moment," Giovanni said as he walked to a side table and deftly extracted a bottle from the bag, placing the other two on the table. Opening the bottle, he poured two glasses, then recorked it. He reached over and extracted a bottle from a crock, opened it, and poured a third glass. Taking all three glasses, he returned, handing them in turn to Désirée, Rachel, and Alphons, who raised an eyebrow. "Aren't you drinking, Giovanni?"

Giovanni gave him an elaborate shrug. "Not yet, my friend. I must oversee the final preparation of the *Bollo Maimon,* and I can't entrust that to apprentices who have never even seen it before! Why don't you take the ladies outside? Introduce them to Summer. We already have several plates of antipasto out there, and the main meal should start in about half an hour."

Alphons' face lit with pleasure. "*Bollo Maimon*? I haven't had that in years!"

Giovanni gave a smiling shrug. "Young 'Sandro has influenced me, and demanded that it be served with what he calls *whipped cream,*" the last two words were in English. "Having tasted it, I think he is right; it should work well," he gave a last, histrionic, shrug. "But I must be away! I have apprentices to terrorize," he smiled, bowed, and returned to the worktable.

Désirée found herself chuckling. "Is he always so, I don't know, larger than life? Like a player on the stage?"

Alphons grinned. "Yes, he is. He is also one of the best cooks I have ever met. You know, he corresponds with *Maestro* Montiño in Madrid?"

Rachel gasped. "Phillip IV's master cook? I thought he was dead!"

"No, just retired. He and Giovanni have been trading letters for several years since *Maestro* Montiño's retirement. But come," he waved them through a door, "let me introduce you to our hosts."

Walking out the door, Désirée was surprised to see that the landing was actually level with a large, grassy area. *The slope on this land must be fierce,* she thought as Alphons led them toward two women, one in her twenties, one in her thirties or forties. Out of the corner of her eye she caught a glimpse of Maria Bergmannin.

Alphons stopped about six feet away from the younger woman.

"Alphons!" she greeted him, "I am *so* glad you could join us, and bring your friends. Please, introduce us." The shift to English was a bit jarring, but both Rachel and Désirée spoke down-time English.

"Of course," Alphons responded. "Summer, this is my good friend Désirée d'Anvers, and her companion Rachel Laurids, from Antwerp. Désirée, Rachel, this is Summer Eckerlin, one of the partners in this venture." Both Désirée and Rachel curtsied.

Summer was shaking her head in what Désirée thought was bemusement. "I'm glad to meet both of you, and I hope you enjoy yourselves tonight." Turning to Alphons, she said, "Let me introduce my guest, Martha Wright. She's a guidance counselor at the Middle School. Martha, this is Master Alphons Verbannen, and his guests Désirée d'Anvers and Rachel Laurids."

The older woman stuck out her hand, which Alphons took and shook. "Glad to meet all of you," she said. "Ah, Mist...er, Master Verbannen, might I have a couple minutes of your time?"

Alphons smiled and nodded. "Of course. But, please, call me Alphons." He gave a slight, deprecating bow. "Everyone in Grantville does."

Martha nodded. "Thanks, Alphons, and call me Martha. So, I wanted..." she stopped as Alphons raised both hands.

"Martha, please! Let me settle Désirée and Rachel first, since I suspect they will wish to talk with others while we converse."

Martha looked a bit flustered, but recovered quickly. "Of course! Sorry, ladies, I should have known better," she said with a wry grin. "Woman on a mission and all that. Talk soon, Alphons."

Alphons nodded and led them to Maria, who was standing with a couple in their twenties. *Woman on a mission,* Désirée thought. *What a strange phrase!*

"Désirée, Rachel! I am *so* glad you were able to come." Maria shifted her gaze to Alphons. "Did that Wright harpy waylay you?"

Alphons choked on a laugh. "You might say that, Maria. I believe I need to return so she can complete her ambush. Do you know exactly why she is here and what Summer's up to?"

The man laughed. "It's Sandy being Sandy, Alphons, and Summer trying to fix things. Sorry." He turned to Désirée and Rachel. "I'm Paul Riddell, and this is my fiancée Birgitte Herdfeuer," he held out his hand, which Désirée, then Rachel, took and shook.

Glancing back at Alphons, he said "Apparently, Sandy has been given the left foot of fellowship by the Home Ec teachers." Spotting Désirée's confusion, he continued. "The middle school requires all students to take either Home Economics—cooking, sewing, household management—or Shop classes—woodworking, metal working, and the like. Usually, girls take Home Ec, while boys take Shop. Sandy's father managed to get him into Home Ec, where he proceeded to humiliate the teachers by being a better cook, and not being quiet about it. They've told the administration that he is *not* welcome back. And, while they can't actually stop him from taking the course, they can make his life hell."

Alphons rolled his eyes while chuckling. "I can just imagine! Uh, Paul, 'left foot of fellowship'?"

Birgitte grinned. "One of those weird, up-time sayings of Paul's. The right hand of fellowship is a handclasp that says 'Welcome,' while the left foot of fellowship is a boot in the ass that says 'Begone.'"

Désirée cracked up laughing. "It's a most evocative saying! I must remember it," she said smiling. "And is this master of irritation with us? I desire to meet one who can inflict such annoyance upon his teachers, and yet inspire such enterprise as we see here."

Paul laughed. "He should be here soon. He's probably showering after his workout."

Désirée understood what showering was, but, "Workout? What, pray tell, is that?"

"Uh," Paul hesitated, "he's been at the gym—that's a *salle des armes*—for the past two hours."

Désirée frowned slightly. "I had thought that he was training as a cook? Why wouldst he be engaged at a *salle des armes*? Surely, a future master cook has no need of a warrior's skills."

Paul shrugged. "I have my suspicions as to why, but feel free to ask him yourself if you wish." Turning to Alphons, he said, "We'll take care of Désirée and Rachel while you go and slay the harpy." Alphons chuckled, nodding, and turned to go to his fate. "Come on ladies, let's sit down and dig into the antipasto before it's all gone."

As Paul and Birgitte led the way over to a long table with benches, Maria dropped back. In a quiet voice, she said in Flemish "I'm sorry, Rachel, but tonight's dinner isn't kosher. They just don't have the resources to build a kosher kitchen right now, although I know Sandy wants one."

Rachel shrugged. "That doesn't bother me. Well, not too much. I have had to eat a lot of non-kosher meals in my life." She sighed, "It's the cost of passing as Catholic."

Maria nodded. "I understand," she said, giving Rachel a quick hug. "Hopefully things will get better soon." She shifted her gaze to Désirée. "And you need to know that both Paul and Birgitte know something about your...'adventures,' last summer."

"How?"

Maria smiled. "I told them." At Désirée's alarmed look, she continued, "Oh, not everything, but they already knew about Alphons working for the *Veedor General*; that came up last winter after Alphons was arrested for murder."

"What?!?!"

Maria looked at her, then sighed. "Why doesn't it surprise me that he didn't mention it in his letters?" She let out a sigh. "Alphons was arrested, but we knew he didn't do it. The person who did, died conveniently of apoplexy." She stopped for a moment. "What you need to understand is that Paul, nice young man that he is, is also the head of military intelligence in Grantville. And I work for him, as does Birgitte."

At Désirée's stunned look, Maria explained. "Grantville is worth protecting, but we aren't insane about it. Feel free to send letters to the *Veedor General*, but I'd suggest sending them via Rachel's uncle. We already have an agreement with Alphons to send messages to the *Veedor General* if needed. We may ask you to do the same if Alphons isn't available."

Désirée was shaking her head in disbelief. "I...I..."

Maria nodded. "Yes, it's a bit more than you expected. But," and here her face grew solemn, "it's not a one-way deal. If you, or the *Veedor General*, need something from us and it doesn't compromise our security, we'll give it to you. Now," she said, rubbing her hands together, "let's see what's for dinner!"

* * *

Several hours later, after walking home, Désirée asked Alphons about Paul. "How are you managing to work with Paul and Maria?"

Alphons leaned back, snagged a bottle, and poured out several glasses of xérès, handing her one. "I don't actually *work* with them," he said, taking a sip, then shrugging. "They already knew I had worked for the *Veedor General* and, after some events, they told me that they don't care, as long as I don't break any of their laws."

Désirée sipped her drink and thought about that. "Maria told me about her and Paul, and maybe wanting me to send Don Luis a message should you not be available."

Alphons shrugged. "They want what they call *back channels*; ways to communicate with people outside of the normal diplomatic routes. I have already sent several messages to Don Luis with their blessings."

Désirée tilted her head. "Doesn't that create a conflict of loyalties?"

Alphons drained his glass, then refilled it, before answering. "Yes and no. I am still loyal to Spain and the Archduchess. But I am here as a merchant, not an intelligencer. Although in some situations, there isn't much difference between the two." He looked deep into his glass. "And the longer I am here, the more I find myself adopting their ways and attitudes."

Désirée thought about that as she tasted her own drink. "And what will you do if the interests of Spain and Grantville come to be at odds with each other?"

She could see Alphons pondering the question, and gave him time to think, wondering how he would answer. Finally, he sighed. "I don't know, Désirée. It would have to depend on the particulars of such a situation."

Thuringen Gardens, Grantville
Saturday, June 12, 1632, 2:05 p.m.

Alphons sat in his chair, calmly enjoying his favorite wine and trying to sort out his feelings. He *thought* things were going well with Désirée, but he was finding it extremely difficult to keep up the pretense of being merely a friend; something they both knew was not what he actually felt. *Still,* he thought as he twirled his wine glass slowly, watching the sunlight make patterns on the table, *I* am *learning somewhat more of what she truly is, as, I hope, she is of me.*

With a sigh, he took a sip and returned to the latest letter from his father, automatically translating the family code. *So, father enjoys the sewing machine I sent him? Hah! He will have it apart and in production within the year!*

Alphons let his eyes scan the next paragraph, schooling his face to show only mild interest rather than the stab of fear that ran through him. The words—*Your feckless cousin Antonio may be going on a Grand Tour in your direction with five or six friends in late July or early August.*—were innocuous, unless you knew the context. Cousin Antonio, or Don Antonio Manuel Miguel de Godelleta, was his uncle's youngest son, who had joined the Army of Flanders in 1627 as a *particular* and worked, quietly, for the *Veedor General.* What the words *meant*, however, were that there were five or six *tercios* of the Army of Flanders on their way.

Alphons put the letter down and took a careful sip. *Can the Americans defeat five or six tercios,* he pondered. He hadn't been at the Battle of the Crapper, but he had talked with a number of people who had. One tercio had been shattered in about five minutes by fewer than three hundred of the Americans and their allies.

More wine followed as he tried to remember how many troops the NUS had, at least troops armed with up-time weapons. *Hmm, at least two thousand by now, possibly more. Add in the cavalry, APCs, and other troops and...* The numbers, and odds, swirled in his head, finally settling on a realization that they could easily defeat six tercios and, probably, as many as ten.

Alphons gave a short nod, then went back to the letter. *Antonio says they may be joined by two more friends later on. If they do show up and you happen to see them, try to keep them out of trouble if at all possible.* He put the letter down and rubbed his temples. *Keep them out of trouble, Father? They're dead men if all they have is eight tercios!*

He reached for his wine and finished it off, signaling Anna for a refill. *Blast! Désirée was right to ask me about conflicts of loyalty! But, if all they're sending is eight tercios...* Alphons reached into his bag and pulled out paper, ink, and a new, steel-tipped, pen. *Now, how to get this information to Paul and Maria without being seen?* He started to chuckle. *Oh, yes, Claes Töpfer should be at church tomorrow. I'll just slip it inside his tunic.*

Dashing off a quick note, he started on the longer letter to his father. He was already writing the second paragraph when his fresh glass arrived. *Hmm, how to tell Father that those tercios will be annihilated? Ah, yes, I need to send him, and the* Veedor General, *information on NUS troops. At best, Don Luis will abort the mission. If not, well, I'm certain that Father can profit from their downfall.*

Verbannen House
Monday, June 14, 1632, 6:04 p.m.

Alphons sat at his desk and smiled as he read the anonymous letter that had been delivered earlier. *I knew Maria would figure it out!* He quickly shuffled through the pages, skimming them. *My, my! She* is *being generous.* Force structure breakdowns, tables of organization, lists of weapons, and *all* of it from publicly available sources, like newspaper articles.

He looked at the lists of weapons and frowned. *Looks like she wants to downplay the effectiveness of some of these. Only* ten *shots a minute? I* know *some will do twenty.* He leaned back in thought, before shrugging. *Oh, well,* he snorted, *even* ten *will be viewed as an exaggeration. This is going to take hours to rewrite so, dinner first, I think.*

* * *

Désirée walked into the front parlor that Alphons was using as an office, holding two glasses of wine. Carefully setting a chilled glass of the Franconian down on the desk, she took a chair and examined Alphons, brow creasing. *He's hiding something.* "So, what *aren't* you telling me?"

She saw something flash over his face.

"Ah...well...just some normal business, but a trifle hurried."

She sipped wine while she examined his face. "Alphons, if you have *any* hope of being *anything* more than a friend, don't *ever* lie to me. I've had too much experience with that, and no wish to deal with it ever again."

Alphons sighed and reached for his glass, considering how to respond. Finally, he shrugged. "I had a letter from my father two days ago telling me that between five and eight tercios are coming this way." Désirée felt herself pale.

"I have no doubt that the Americans will smash them, even if they are caught unawares; their army is too strong, and tercios move too slowly. So," Alphons closed his eyes, took a deep breath, and opened them again, spearing her with his gaze, "I warned Paul they were coming."

Désirée drew in a sharp breath, then let it out slowly. "Are you *certain* the Americans will win?"

Alphons chuckled ruefully. "Certain? No, nothing is certain in war. What I am certain about is that they defeated a single tercio with under three hundred troops, in five minutes, and they now have over two thousand. Désirée," he leaned forward, "it will be a slaughter and, for my sins, my favorite cousin is coming with them. I just hope," he said quietly, "that Antonio lives."

Désirée found herself nodding. "I will pray for him." She sipped her wine and considered Alphons. "But that doesn't account for the smile on your face when I walked in."

"That was from seeing you."

"Alphons..." she growled, slitting her eyes.

He just laughed, and held up the letter he had been reading. "And this. Maria sent me the entire American order of battle with estimates of range and firepower. She suggested that I forward it to the *Veedor General*."

Désirée thought that through. "Payback?" she asked. On getting a nod, she continued parsing her thoughts. "So...it probably won't stop the attack, but you will earn favor with Don Luis and, perhaps, others." She sighed. "It seems as if I can take Maria at her word, then."

Summer's Kitchen Store, 105 Water Street, Grantville Sunday, July 4, 1632, 1:35 p.m.

Désirée looked at the scene in front of her and shook her head.

"Bit of a madhouse, isn't it?" Paul Riddell said, as he and Birgitte joined Désirée, Alphons, and Rachel on the street outside the store. There was a large BBQ set up in front of the store, and many people were clamoring for the food they appeared to be giving away.

Désirée gave Paul a quirky smile. "In sooth, it reminds me of a song I heard after the English king had taken the monasteries, causing all of their inhabitants to roam the land."

Paul twitched an eyebrow. "Bedlam Boys?"

Désirée frowned slightly. "If you mean this," she said, taking a breath and starting to sing.

"For to see my Tom O'Bedlam, ten thousand miles I'll travel.

Mad Maudlin walks on dirty toes, for to keep her shoes from gravel.

"If that's the song, then aye, I know it."

Paul laughed. "Oh, my! That's wonderful! I love that song," he said smiling. "Well, we should probably join the line and get some food while the getting is good."

All of them got into line, with Paul ending up next to Alphons. Désirée could just barely hear Paul say "Did you send off that information?" and Alphons' affirmative. *So*, Désirée thought, *the Veedor General has the information, and Paul knows it. I wonder what that means?*

Verbannen House
Friday, July 9, 1632, 9:05 a.m.

Désirée carefully closed the book she had been studying and laid it on the table with a sigh. *I'm bored*, she thought, then started to chortle: the thought of being bored struck her as hilarious. *I've been here for over five weeks, and outside of a bit of shopping, school, and a few visits, I've gone hardly anywhere. It's time to do something different.*

She glanced out the window, seeing the sunlight, then down at her house dress. *I'd best change*, she thought. *I think that up-time cotton dress I bought at the Value Mart should do. After all*, she smiled, *I've only worn it once.* The dress was, by down-time reckoning, more than somewhat scandalous, ending at just below her knees—she had had to alter one of her chemises to go with it—but it was light and didn't irritate her back.

Up in her room, she changed clothes, put on a pair of walking sandals, and grabbed a small basket. Back downstairs in the kitchen where Elsa was working, she said, "I'm heading out for a couple of hours, Elsa. Can I get you anything?"

Elsa glanced up, smiling. "No, we're good. Will you be back for lunch?"

"I should be," Désirée replied. "I have school at 1:00, and I *do* want to eat before then."

Elsa laughed. "I *totally* understand! Have fun."

Désirée smiled as she put on a large, floppy, straw hat, waved goodbye, and left. *Maybe I should go and find out about these Committees of Correspondence that Meester Laurids suggested.*

The Freedom Arches, Grantville
9:55 a.m.

Désirée paused as she entered the Freedom Arches and took in the stares and silence. *Pest! I may have made a mistake coming here*, she thought, taking in the hostile silence. A man, probably an up-timer, given that he was wearing an apron, walked towards her. "Can I help you, ma'am? Do you need directions somewhere?" he asked in up-time English.

"Ah, I was told that this is where I could find the Committees of Correspondence. Several acquaintances have told me that I should seek them out and learn about them and the work they do."

The man smiled at her, and waved a hand encompassing the inside of the building. "And you've found us. I'm Andy Yost, manager of the Arches," he held out his hand, which she shook in the up-time manner.

"I am Désirée d'Anvers."

At his slightly confused look, a voice spoke out. "She's a whore, Andy. Probably looking for clients. Look at her clothing and hair."

Désirée glared at the speaker, a tall, well-built, scarred man in his thirties. *Hard*, she thought, *Probably a mercenary. Only one way to deal with this*, she thought as she gave the man a tight smile with no cordiality in it. "That would be *ex*-whore. Not," she looked him up and down, "that you could ever have afforded me, even in your wildest dreams."

He stared at her, then started to smile, finally laughing out loud. "And so, I'm put in my place," he said as he stood up. *Mijn God! He's as tall as Alphons!* He held out a hand. "Ulric Halvorsen."

"Désirée d'Anvers."

"So, Désirée, you're here to find out what the Committees do?" Ulric smiled. "We plot revolution, and look for ways to make our emerging country a better place for all people. But," he waved at a bench, "sit down. Andy," he called out, "can we have a couple of small beers, please, while I give Désirée an overview?"

Andy nodded. "Just don't get used to table service, Ulric." He wandered towards the back of the building, and behind a counter, while Désirée sat down.

"'Table service'? What is that?"

Ulric snorted slightly. "Having our drinks delivered. Normally, we go up to the counter for them."

Désirée nodded in understanding. *Strange, but that's Grantville.* "And so, you say 'revolution'. Of what kind? For I have heard nothing of that, while hearing only good things of many of your activities. 'Tis not what I would have expected."

Ulric shrugged. Before he could say anything, Andy returned with several tankards, placing them on the table. "Thanks, Andy." He returned his gaze to Désirée. "Yes, revolution, but of a quiet type. We promote sanitation, fair employment, and freedom of religion. We help people find decent work. We encourage people to vote, and become active in the political life of their communities. We teach people about equality."

Désirée cocked her head. "Don't the local nobility oppose you? It would seem that you are appropriating their prerogatives."

Ulric snorted. "The *Hochadel* not so much. Some of the *Niederadel*, patricians, and guild masters more so, at least within the New United States. Outside?" he shrugged, "Well, we don't care for now."

Désirée felt the time was right to ask something that had bothered her for several days. "And what if those outside take up arms against Grantville?"

Ulric grinned savagely. "The reactionaries? We would crush them into the ground."

Désirée just looked at him. "And if you faced, say, eight tercios? Could you deny them?"

The grin left Ulric's face. "Girl, tercios move *slowly*. I know, I was in one, and now I'm a sergeant in the NUS army. We would know about them with days to spare. We could take eight of them like that," he snapped his fingers, then leaned back and examined her carefully. "We could probably take ten or twelve with no advance warning, but why would you think of eight?"

Désirée settled her face into a bland expression. "Oh, just an idle thought." She could tell that Ulric didn't believe her. She sighed. "That number might have come up in a passing conversation last Sunday."

Ulric examined her carefully. "Oh? And who was this 'passing conversation' with?"

Désirée realized that Ulric knew the number and was pressing her for her source. "An up-timer, one Paul Riddell. He is, I believe, something in your military."

Ulric just stared at her, then started shaking his head. "You move in more exalted circles than I do if you know Captain Riddell." Ulric examined her closely. "So, shall we talk about how you might work with us?" The next hour and a half were, to Désirée, illuminating.

Verbannen House
Monday, July 12, 1632, 8:25 a.m.

"Rachel?"

Rachel looked up. "Yes?"

"I have visited with the Committees of Correspondence, and there are some people you should meet," Désirée said with a slight smile.

Summer's Kitchen Store
Wednesday, July 14, 1632, 9:05 a.m.

Désirée followed Alphons into the store, smiling at the cheerful tinkling of a bell as he opened the door. Inside, the sound of Voice Of America came over the radio. Earlier that morning, Alphons had asked her if she would come with him and help out. She had shrugged and agreed.

The entrance was on the left-hand side of the storefront, next to Bartoli's Sporting Goods. The store had ample storage and display space, even if it was only sixteen feet across and thirty feet deep, with display shelves on the left-hand side. A counter spanned the right side, with display space behind the counter and the last five feet, right by the window, held two grinding wheels: one horizontal, one vertical.

The next nine feet held three cutting boards, and the wall behind was adorned with different knives. The next section of wall held a large slate listing herbs, spices, cheese, condiments, wines, and their prices. The counter below was empty, save for a weighing scale. The final seven feet of the store had been left open. *I wonder what they are planning on putting in there,* Désirée thought as she took in the sights.

"Hans!" Alphons called out. "I trust you were expecting me?"

"Of course, Master Verbannen. Sandy warned me you would be coming in this morning. I have the sales figures ready for you."

Alphons was shaking his head. "I've told you, Hans, you need to call me 'Alphons.'"

Hans, a man in his early thirties from what Désirée could tell, snorted. "Aye, that you have, but I think I'll wait for a while. So," he took up a sheaf of papers and handed them to Alphons, "here are the figures. Better than I would have thought."

Alphons took the papers and waved Désirée forward. "Désirée, this is Hans Bauer, the senior apprentice here. Hans, this is my good friend Désirée d'Anvers who has agreed to help me with this little exercise."

Désirée held out her hand. "Good to meet you, Hans."

Hans took her hand and shook it, murmuring "A rose by any other name..." in English. "Delighted to meet you, Désirée," he said, switching back to German.

Désirée smiled, then turned to Alphons. "May I see those, please?" He wordlessly handed them to her, and she started skimming. *These* are *good sales, but...* She glanced up at Hans. "Do you have any idea who bought what? Up-timers? Down-timers? Cooks? Groups?"

Hans was nodding. "Not exactly," he said. "We just don't gather that kind of information. In the first week, my impression was that it was mainly up-timers who were buying. That seems to have evened out now, and I believe we are selling more kitchenware to down-timers. We *are* selling a fair amount of fresh pasta, and we have at least twenty clients who have what Sandy calls *standing orders.*"

Hans shifted his gaze to Alphons. "We've also been asked if we can pre-make the sauce we used for the opening and sell that. Several up-timers have asked about tomato sauce. And some people are asking about buying pre-made lasagnas, but in smaller Töpferware that they can return."

Alphons was nodding. "I'll bring those up with Summer and *Maestro* Amendola. Have you been getting any other requests?"

Hans snorted. "Quite a few, actually. I've got a list here for you," he reached under the counter and handed Alphons a sheet of paper. "The one that the most people asked for, and they were all up-timers, was pepperoni. Apparently, it's some type of semi-hard sausage, but..." he shrugged.

Alphons gave him a wry grin. "Up-timers. Who knows if it even exists now."

Verbannen House
9:32 p.m.

Désirée walked into the front room where Alphons was working and handed him a glass of wine, before taking a seat, cradling her own glass. "Thank you. I would have expected you to be in bed already," Alphons said in a querying tone.

Désirée shrugged, wondering how to formulate the questions she had. "I find I have much on my mind."

Alphons cocked his head to the side and sipped his wine while he studied her. "Is there anything I can help you with?"

I think he actually means that, Désirée thought as she sipped her wine. *I have seen him act the fool. I have seen him be a successful merchant, a cold-blooded calculator, and a vengeful killer, but I have no idea what actually motivates him beyond the necessities of the moment.* "Are those the Summer's Kitchen sales figures you're working on?"

Alphons raised an eyebrow in what Désirée assumed was surprise. "Yes. They really are quite interesting. If I extrapolate from these figures, they need to treble, maybe quadruple, some parts of their orders. Probably more for the Parmesan cheese; I still have difficulty believing how much of that they sold."

Désirée nodded. *Do I ask?* She let out a small sigh. "I think I understand *what* you are doing but, what I wanted to ask was *why* you are doing it. I haven't seen you do anything like this for your other clients."

Alphons set his glass down on the table. "No, I haven't, but that is because my other clients are merchants, businesses, or large households. They are quite capable of projecting their own needs and don't need my help. And"—a smile flashed over his face—"they know that I would charge them for any such service."

Désirée raised an eyebrow of her own. "Are you charging Summer's Kitchen?"

Alphons shook his head. "No."

"Why not?"

"Because I like them?" He smiled whimsically. "Well, that is part of it, but only a small part." The smile dissolved. "Do you know why my father left Spain?"

Désirée shook her head in confusion at the apparent change in topic. "No, I don't, but your family name is suggestive."

Alphons chuckled. "Yes, 'banished' is that. My father left because *his* father was more concerned with the *appearance* of honor than with taking care of his people. My father was," he frowned, then smiled, "ah, yes, 'given the left foot of fellowship' by his father; 'banished' as it were.

"Well, my grandfather is dead and my uncle now runs the family estates that are, slowly, recovering. But the only reason they are recovering is because my father sends my uncle money to help rebuild them." Alphons sighed. "Sandy and Summer, and to a lesser extent Helmut, remind me of my father: they both care about and for their people. I admire that and want to encourage it; it is too rare not to," he said ruefully.

Désirée nodded slowly as she thought about what Alphons had said. "Is that why they have apprentices in their thirties?"

"You mean Hans? Yes. From what I understand, he was a pikeman for over a decade, and is now starting a new life. He can do that thanks to Summer's Kitchen. And"—he studied his wineglass—"do you know what their apprenticeship fees are?"

Désirée shook her head, while Alphons started to smile. "Nothing. They charge no fees whatsoever. Désirée, they *live* the ideal of honor, and I want to help them out. I couldn't live with myself if I didn't. *That's* why I am helping them."

* * *

As Désirée lay in bed later on, trying to sleep, her mind kept circling back to her conversation with Alphons. *Honor? I've only heard that word from bastards who use it to justify destroying people,* she thought, but then relented. *No, not quite true. The* Veedor General *is honorable.* Meester *Laurids is honorable. And I think Alphons is.* She sighed, and tried to find a more comfortable position. *I hope I'm right.*

Summer's Kitchen Workshop
Tuesday, August 3, 1632, 9:05 a.m.

Désirée strolled through the third-floor kitchen of the workshop, seeing Giovanni talking with several young apprentices, his signature theatrics apparent in waving hands and exaggerated expressions. She wasn't there for Giovanni, though, so she didn't interrupt. She had awoken that morning with the feeling that she needed to talk with someone, and Birgitte and

Maria were away. She *could* have talked with Rachel, she supposed, but she didn't think that Rachel had the right kind of experience to understand her quandary. *Summer,* she thought, *might.* She had called Summer half an hour ago and been invited over.

She was still smiling at Giovanni's antics as she walked outside, spotting Summer on one of the benches reading. As she came closer, Summer looked up and smiled. "Hi, Désirée. Want something to drink?"

"My thanks, but no," Désirée said as she sat opposite Summer.

"So," Summer said, "what can I do for you?"

Désirée felt her thoughts flit off into the aether. "I, uh, well, I had a hope that you could advise me on a personal matter."

"Alphons?"

Désirée nodded. "I find myself conflicted in his regard."

"How so?" Summer started to frown. "Is he being an asshole?"

Désirée laughed. "Nay, he is the very model of a gentleman. It's that I find myself loath to live off his charity and, well, I find my liking of him increasing as I come to know him better. He is a man of parts."

Summer was nodding. "So, then, what do you want? Do you want to marry him?"

"God's love, no!" Désirée exclaimed, then caught her scattered thoughts. "At the least, his father would stand opposed, and it would create a rift between them that I would not willingly cause." She took a deep breath, "And I have no wish to be any man's chattel, however fond I am."

"I hear you!"

Désirée was feeling confused. "And yet, didn't you wed last year?"

Summer grinned. "Sure I did. But under our laws, men don't own their wives." A more serious look replaced her amusement. "And while I'll tell *you* this, I'll deny it if you repeat it to *anyone*...I didn't marry Bob because I fell madly in love. I married Bob to escape from my life."

Summer paused. "It was awful after the Ring of Fire. Just awful. And my life wasn't great *before* that." She looked down at her hands. "I was...kind of between things. I hadn't really figured out where I fit or what I was going to do." She looked back up. "So when everything changed, just so totally changed, it was all 'oh, Summer can do this and Summer can do that' with no one asking me what I thought about it.

"Don't get me wrong," she continued, "I like Bob, and I respect him. But what was really important, and what was different from every other person in my life right then, was that he liked me for *me*. Not for what I could do for him, even though he was feeling really lost himself, and it probably would have been easy just to see me as a solution to his problems, but that's not how he thought about things. He cared about what *I* felt and what *I* wanted. He made me smile, and eventually he made me laugh, and I hadn't done that in so, so long.

"He's a good man, but...limited. I know his limits, and I can work with them. I've even come to love him in my own way, especially given"—she said waving at the workshop—"his support for this venture. I truly believe that he wants me to become what I can be. He may not *understand* either me or Sandy, but he does his best to support us, and that's worth a *lot* in my books."

Désirée found herself nodding. "Aye, to have a man who would seek to support rather than dominate; whose hand was outstretched in aid and comfort rather than in threat...Yes, I can see the appeal."

Summer looked at her. "And do you think Alphons might be that for you?"

Désirée shrugged. "I don't know. It may be possible, but his father's dis-approval wouldn't change, even so. To say nothing of my own...aversion."

"Well, maybe you don't need to *actually* get married; just *act* as if you were. Up-time, we had all sorts of couples who lived together without being married—we called it 'shacking up'. Hey, even I did that for a while. But the important point is that under West Virginia law, which is what we have here in the NUS, there is no common-law marriage. Even if you lived together for twenty years, you wouldn't be *legally* married."

Désirée felt her eyes growing large. "But...but the Church? What would they do?"

Summer chuckled. "Talk to Father Larry about that. He'd try to convince you to get married, but, if he couldn't, he'd want to see some type of legal agreement to take care of any children. And to ensure they're raised Catholic." She rolled her eyes. "Of course," her eyes grew playful, "some of the old biddies—Irene Flannery springs to mind—will take a stern, disapproving, and probably *vocal* stance against it, but you can't please everyone."

Summer became serious again. "It's an option, Désirée. If you went with it, you would need to work out a co-habitation contract with Alphons. And you would have to put up with a certain amount of social stigma." She shrugged. "Just something to think about."

Verbannen House
8:53 p.m.

The movie had ended over twenty minutes ago, and Hans and Elsa had shooed the children off to bed. Rachel had gone up soon after, citing an early morning appointment, leaving Alphons and Désirée alone. The silence was becoming oppressive. "Alphons, could you pour us drinks?" Désirée asked, breaking the awkward silence.

"Of course! Xérès?" At her nod, he got up, went over to the sideboard, and filled two glasses. "Here you are." He handed her a small glass and settled back in his chair. "Did you want to talk about something?"

Désirée nodded. "Yes. About us, and where we might go."

Alphons raised an eyebrow. "I was under the impression that you wished us only to be friends. Was I mistaken?"

Désirée gave him a wry grin. "Maybe?" She sighed and took a sip of her drink. "There are...practicalities that must be considered."

Alphons caught and held her eyes. "You *do* know that my father married 'beneath him'—well, at least according to my grandfather?"

Désirée nodded. "But your mother was the daughter of a successful merchant. Not," her eyes flashed, "a *whore*. Your father would never countenance such a match, nor would the Church."

Alphons sighed. "Father Mazarre might..."

Désirée huffed, "Don't be ridiculous, Alphons. Oh," she said, waving a hand, "he might overlook my prior 'occupation', but in the face of paternal disapproval?" She shook her head. "No. And there are too many Jesuits there for him to overlook them. Besides *that*, he is a parish priest cut adrift in time, with no power, regardless of what he might believe."

Alphons opened his mouth, then, slowly, closed it. "I fear you are correct."

"Good, you recognize that problem."

Alphons grimaced. "Of course I do. I also," he regarded her solemnly, "recognize the *other* problem, which you haven't mentioned. I'm besotted with you, but I know that is an attraction to an illusion created in my own mind. I do not know *you*: not as well as I would like." He regarded her carefully, then sighed. "I would really like to know *you*, rather than the illusions."

Désirée just looked at him, then, slowly, started to smile. *Maybe this could work out.*

Verbannen House
Wednesday, August 4, 1632, 7:35 a.m.

"Are you *certain* you want to do this, Rachel?" Désirée asked, spoon paused in its trip to her mouth.

Rachel shrugged. "Certain? No." Her eyes speared Désirée. "But the chance; the opportunity, to be what I am? I can live, and support myself openly, as a Jew, and *that* is important." She leaned forward. "You *know* how important that is, Désirée. 'To thine own self be true, and it must follow, as the night the day, thou canst not then be false to any man'."

Désirée rolled her eyes. "Shakespeare? An over-rated wordsmith in my opinion! Still..." she shook her head. "I will miss you. But,"—she pointed the spoon at Rachel—"I expect you to visit. Often."

Rachel smiled. "Of course!"

Verbannen House
Monday, August 16, 1632, 11:15 p.m.

Désirée was tossing in her bed, not able to sleep. She knew that some of her difficulties were because she was missing Rachel but...the majority were not. She shifted over onto her back, thankful that she could do that now, while her mind went back to the Croat raid.

She had been in the Summer's Kitchen store, talking with Hans, when she heard the radio say, "There's a raid!" Hans had looked around, and yelled out, "Lock everything down. We need to get out of here, now!"

Désirée had been confused, but Hans had led her over to the second floor of Bartoli's Sporting Goods, saying, "This is our station. Do you have a gun?"

"A *gun*? No!"

Hans just looked at her and shook his head. "Fine. Deal with any wounded." He looked out the window, shook his head, and swore. "What the fuck is she doing here?" Désirée went to the window, and saw Summer sprinting down the street, carrying two guns, before she entered the store and disappeared from sight.

A moment later, Summer ran into the second-floor room, looking around. "Hans, you know how to fire a rifle?" He nodded, and Summer tossed one of the guns she was carrying at him, before pulling off a bag she was carrying. "Ammo," she said, pointing to the bag. "Désirée, do you know how to shoot?"

Désirée shook her head. "No."

Summer snorted. "No time like the present, girlfriend." She pulled a small gun out and handed it to Désirée. "This is a Glock. Seventeen shots. It's simple: point and shoot. I've got four more mags ready." At Désirée's confused look, she snorted. "Magazines. I'll show you. Just aim and pull the trigger." Désirée nodded.

It had been...well, the word "surreal" encompassed the experience. She rolled onto her side as the memories flowed. Seeing a single man stare down the combined might of the raiders, and then watching them melt, like snow in the hot sun, as gunfire roared from the buildings, her own included. She had kept shooting until all she heard was clicks, and Summer carefully took the gun from her hands, saying, "It's over, Désirée."

"Holy Mary, Mother of God, what have I done," she whispered and crossed herself as the cries of wounded men and horses reached her ears, accompanied by a growing stench.

She felt Summer taking her chin and moving her head so that she was looking at Summer's face, and not the carnage outside. "You did what had to be done to protect all of us."

Hans walked over, rifle in one hand. "She's right, Désirée. Those bastards would have cheerfully slaughtered us all, and don't ever think otherwise." His eyes flicked to Summer. "The Workshop?"

She nodded. "I distributed the rest of our guns, and put Adolph in charge of the defense." A smile flickered over her face. "When last seen, Giovanni was wearing a rapier and dagger and waving a huge cleaver, threatening to turn any attacker into sausage meat."

Désirée found herself smiling at the thought of the voluble Italian cook. Then her mind hiccupped. "Oh my God! Alphons!" Her mind generated all sorts of images of Alphons lying dead, and her heart started to race in panic.

Summer looked at her. "He's at the warehouse in Saalfeld. We haven't heard any reports of Saalfeld being hit, so he should be safe." Désirée felt a flash of relief when she heard that.

Returning to her sleepless present, squirming over to her other side, Désirée wondered. *And why would I be so...concerned about Alphons? He can take care of himself, and it's not like we are married!* That was, she would admit, but only in the deepest recesses of her mind, being unfair to Alphons.

She sighed, and rolled over onto her back, thoughts roiling. *Do I love him?* She jeered at herself, *What do I know about love, outside its per hour cost?* A sigh escaped her lips. *Still, I do care for him, for his well-being, probably more than I should.* That thought sparked a memory of her earlier conversations with Summer and Alphons. *Maybe, just maybe, there is a way out of this impasse, but I need to test it*, she thought, before throwing back the covers.

* * *

Alphons woke when he heard his bedroom door opening. His right hand slid, slowly, under his pillow where he had a dagger secreted for emergencies. He heard a slight, feminine, chuckle. "I don't think you'll need that, Alphons."

Verbannen House
Tuesday, August 17, 1632, 6:45 a.m.

Elsa was shaking her head as she watched Alphons bounce—bounce!—off as he headed to the warehouse. *I haven't seen him that happy since he heard Désirée was coming! And*, she thought as Désirée came into the dining room, *think of the Devil...*

"Ah, Elsa...I'm heading over to the Workshop. I need to talk with Summer. I should be back by six, but," Desiree said, "don't wait dinner on me."

7:15 p.m.

"Alphons, can we talk? In private?" Désirée asked with an uncertain note in her voice.

"Hmmm?" He looked up from where he was finishing off his crème caramel, another one of the recipes that Sandy was starting to popularize. "Oh, yes, certainly. A glass of wine?" He saw her nod, and topped off both of their glasses. "Maybe the porch? It's probably our best bet if you want privacy."

She nodded and picked up her wine glass, along with a small portfolio. When they exited the house and got to the porch, Alphons waved to a long bench. "So, what did you want to talk about, Désirée?"

She twitched a smile. "Well, first of all, I legally changed my name today. 'Désirée' was a name imposed on me when I came to *De Oprechte Mens*, and I have absolutely no desire to keep it."

Alphons nodded. "Are you going back to your birth name, then?"

She shook her head. "No. My family is dead; attainted for heresy and executed," she saw Alphons wince. "I will not try to reclaim that heritage. Anything I might have inherited from them—the estate, the business interests—is in the pockets of the Inquisitors, who confiscated it for the costs of their torture and trial. I can only pray that those bastards end up in the Hell they so richly deserve."

She realized how upset she was and struggled to control her breathing. "No, I will not go back, only forward. I am here, in Grantville, and I have the opportunity to be reborn. Indeed," she smiled, "I took a leaf from your father's book and chose the last name of Herboren—Reborn. For my use name, well, it actually came from Hans at the Summer's Kitchen shop. When we were introduced, he mumbled 'a Rose by any other name'. So, that is my new name: Rose Herboren."

Alphons smiled. "It suits you. Rose." He raised his glass in salute, then cocked his head, considering her. "Was that all you wanted to talk about?"

She twisted her wine glass, then drank and placed the glass on the arm of the bench. "No," she looked Alphons in the eye. "We both know that your father would never countenance us marrying, and I would not offer you such a...fraught choice. But," she drew on her inner strength, "I find myself desirous of seeing what *we* might become, even if we were *not* married."

At Alphons' raised eyebrows, she continued. "Apparently, there is a venerable American tradition known as 'shacking up.' From what Summer tells me, it was rampant in the up-time, and involved living as husband and wife without actually being married. Some of their states *did* codify it in law as 'common-law' marriage, but West Virginia was not one of those states."

She chuckled at Alphons' slightly croggled look. "Alphons, what I am suggesting is that we explore the potential of operating as if we were husband and wife, but with no marriage; our relationship will be bounded by contract, rather than custom and Church law." Rose watched Alphons' face carefully, seeing him move from confusion to understanding. It was not, after all, as if there were no precedents to what she was proposing.

Slowly, Alphons nodded. "I would guess, then, that any negotiations would be over the contract? Do you, by chance," he asked with some irony, "happen to *have* a proposed contract?" *Did I misread her? Is she going to try to take advantage of me?* He wondered as he waited for her reply.

Rose reached into her portfolio. "Yes, I do. Here you are," she said as she handed him ten sheets of paper.

Alphons took them, worrying that he had made a serious mistake. "Thank you." As he read, he was conscious of Rose watching him closely. *This contract*, he thought, *is written in an exceedingly strange manner.* At the start of each section, there was a statement of intent, followed by a statement of assumptions. Following both of those, were the actual clauses.

When he saw the heading of Household Maintenance, he frowned. *This is where the gouging usually happens*, he thought. *Wait! What?* Under "Intent" he read, *The intent is to share all expenses evenly.* His eyes flicked to the "Assumptions," where he noted that Rose mentioned she did not, currently, have the income to support her share. The clause itself stated, *Each signatory shall contribute no greater than 30 percent of their net income to household expenses, and any particular lack of contribution shall not be charged against them for future repayment.* Alphons found himself nodding. *Smart!*

A quick look showed him that each section, and clause, was similar: an intention to evenly split all expenses, but a realistic take on what was currently possible. And the clauses were eerily similar in stating that control of resources—land, stock, investments, and monies—were to be maintained by each, without any possibility of claims by the other unless described in the contract or freely given. Alphons finished reading, then returned to the first page, scanning each line carefully.

* * *

Rose watched Alphons with increasing trepidation as he reread the contract. *Was I wrong about him? Does he want to control me as so many others have?* After some time, he laid the sheaf of papers down. "That"—he flicked a finger at the papers—"was not what I was expecting."

Exasperated, Rose retorted, "Alphons, I want to be your *partner*, not your extortioner. It seems only fair to me that we split costs on everything, including children, were we to be so blessed." *As if I would have children without my choice, but he doesn't need to know that.*

Alphons was nodding. "Yes, I agree. The contract is, in my opinion, more than fair and guards both of our interests. I would be happy to sign it. Let us," he said with a blinding smile, "see what we might become."

I was right, she exulted, feeling a matching smile growing. *And now that the ground is prepared, we can begin the actual work.*

The Brezelgeist Romance
David Hankins

Summer 1631

So far, life as Herr Abrabanel's spy primarily involved walking too many miles without a horse. As a career coachman, Dominik wasn't used to traveling on his own feet over long distances. He missed his horses. He missed his coach. But he understood the need to arrive in Dresden with nothing but a knapsack and a smile.

The road from Grantville had been pleasant enough, late spring in Germany nearly hiding the scars of over a decade of war, but it had been lonely, too. Dominik liked having company. He'd been a widower for two decades, yet over the years he'd always found someone to pass the time with, even if they were just passengers. Now he was starting a career that was, by definition, a solitary one. True, he'd never pursued marriage again after Greta, but the possibility of finding someone to share his life with had always been there.

Not anymore. Spies work in the dark. They don't have families. Dominik was surprised at the sharp pang of loss for something he hadn't actually had; the loss of a possibility. Yet it was a sacrifice he was willing to make. He'd spent a month with the Americans in Grantville while Herr Abrabanel arranged his apprenticeship. In that time, he'd come to believe in the rightness of helping these strangers from the future survive and thrive in what the Americans called the Thirty Years' War.

Dominik pushed his tumbling thoughts into the background as he passed through Dresden's walled gates and stepped onto its cobbled streets. It was nice to be back in a proper city, to feel the stone beneath his boots and smell the unmistakable smells of thousands of humans living on top of each other. Tanneries and bakeries, spices and horse sweat. The uniquely urban concoction made Dominik yearn for home. Not the German farm he was born on, but Amsterdam, where he and Greta had escaped to when they were just a couple of love-struck kids. Amsterdam was where they'd built a life, he'd become a coachman, and they'd dreamed the grand dreams of the young and foolish. God, he missed her.

He drew a deep breath and walked on. After twenty years, the sorrow was like an old friend.

The mid-morning streets were tight and cramped, and Dominik wove around carts and pedestrians. Then he turned a corner and his destination, the Residenz Schloss, rose above the surrounding courtyard like a Renaissance goddess. Decorative spires reached for the sky. High windows and ostentatious gilding made the residence of John George, Elector of Saxony, a true wonder to behold.

Dominik only knew the basics of spycraft and deception—that was the point of his apprenticeship here—but it didn't take much to talk his way past the bored palace guards. He headed for the kitchens. He was to meet a man named Herr Kleingard, a master spy for the Abrabanel family's extensive network, who had been feeding them information for decades.

When Dominik pushed his way through white-washed kitchen doors, he was assaulted by a riot of noise. Lunch prep was in full swing. He inhaled deeply, and his stomach growled. But before his nose identified more than fresh pretzels and frying sausage, a sturdy middle-aged woman stepped into his path. She wore a green dirndl covered by a well-used white apron.

Her striking green eyes roved over him like a hound eying a steak. Her blonde hair was braided into a crown, but Dominik barely noticed. He was transfixed by her eyes. They were the same sea-green that Greta's had been. This stranger moved with the subtle grace of a woman who knew exactly how beautiful she was, like a Valkyrie descended from the heavens.

Dominik suddenly found it hard to breathe.

"Hello, handsome," she purred, "What brings you to my kitchen?"

"I...uh..."

"Oh, he's a shy one," she called over her shoulder to the kitchen at large. "I like 'em shy." She stepped close, and Dominik backed away. He didn't get far. The open door behind him clipped his heel. He stumbled and caught himself on her arm that was suddenly there, offering support. It was a solid arm, firm with muscle from a lifetime of labor. It was also warm and smooth under his touch, and his heart gave a quick two-step flutter.

What was wrong with him? He never reacted like this when he met a woman, no matter how beautiful. Regardless, he met her gaze and briefly wondered if the poets were right. Could you drown in a woman's eyes? The last woman who'd looked at him like that had been Greta. Twenty years was a long time.

Bubbling laughter erupted from the other cooks. "Found yourself another lover, Hildegard?" a young woman asked as she kneaded dough. "He looks completely smitten!"

A girl who couldn't have been older than twelve looked up from the pan she was scrubbing. "At least this one's prettier than the last." This spurred a wave of coarse laughter and ribald assessments of Dominik's appearance. He'd always considered himself rather plain. Mid-forties with brown hair, brown eyes, and a neatly trimmed beard that was only beginning to show grey. He'd never heard anyone describe him as roguishly handsome before. He *was* wearing his coachman's livery, but it was dirty from his travels. Nothing to gawk over.

Hildegard moved closer, nearly but not quite pressing against him as his back bumped against the now-closed door. "Yes," she murmured, looking him up and down. "You do have the look of a rogue about you. Did you drop by for a little snack, or for something...more?"

What? No! Dominik was a good Christian man. He wasn't going to be seduced by a woman he'd just met simply because she had dazzling eyes. He drew a deep breath, trying to focus on the smell of fresh, hot pretzels.

Hildegard was so close that all he smelled was her. It was the smell of good, honest sweat overlaid by some cooking spice that was rich and unidentifiable. It brought to mind Christmas feasts and candlelit dinners.

He realized that his hand was still on her arm. He let go and straightened, closing his fist over the memory of warmth. His cheeks burned. He had to clear his throat twice before he could speak. "My name is Dominik Wagner. I am looking for Herr Kleingard?" He didn't mean that to come out as a question. "I was told to inquire in the kitchen."

She cocked her head, her gaze turning more curious than amorous. "Nobody here by that name, but perhaps the Hofmeister knows him." Hildegard turned and beckoned with a crooked finger. "Follow me."

Her hips swayed as she wove through the kitchen, headed for the door to the courtyard. Dominik followed, keeping his eyes firmly averted. He blushed again when someone whistled at his own departing backside. These women were entirely too forward.

* * *

The flagstone courtyard was large and relatively unoccupied. A woodsman and his son were unloading a cart of firewood. A handful of servants strode purposefully across the open space. Two washerwomen with heavy bundles curtsied as they passed two nobles holding an intense conversation in the sunshine. One noble was a thin, dour-faced man wearing a dark, well-made outfit, while the other was shorter and rounder and more bedecked with gold braid. From their postures, Dominik assumed the shorter man, though younger, was the senior noble.

Hildegard turned left outside the kitchen and sashayed toward an herb garden in the corner of the courtyard. Tucked into the corner behind the garden was a cluster of tall decorative bushes, which Dominik assumed hid a servant's door. She led him down a narrow path between rows of herbs, glancing over her shoulder. She didn't look at Dominik but scanned the courtyard.

He didn't see a door behind the bushes. Abruptly, Hildegard slipped into the shadows and grabbed his wrist, pulling him into hiding.

"What do you think—" he started, but she clapped a hand over his mouth and slammed him against the wall. Her body was warm and soft, but her hand over his face was calloused and strong. She was nearly his height and gazed hard into his eyes. Her expression was no longer sultry.

"Rule number one," she hissed, "Never use Herr Kleingard's name in mixed company. Don't you know anything about contact protocols?"

Dominik tried to say, "Contact what?" but it came out as a mumble. His eyes must have shown his confusion. Hildegard's lips pursed.

"I knew who you were the second you walked in. The only reason I agreed to train you is because Herr Abrabanel said that you were a natural spy. But if you can't even handle a basic first contact, I may as well just kill you now and save everybody the time!"

Dominik's eyes bulged, and he squirmed. He froze when something small and sharp pressed against his ribs.

"Rule number two: Always have a weapon ready." Hildegard raised the blade and waggled it. "Even if it isn't yours."

Dominik's hand flashed to his waist, but only found an empty sheath. She had his utility knife. His gaze flicked from the knife to the woman keeping him pinned. If it came to it, he wasn't entirely sure he could overpower her.

She considered him for a long moment. Her piercing green eyes narrowed. "I'm going to release you. Let's see if you can learn from your mistakes...but consider your words carefully. What you say next will determine your fate."

Hildegard's hand dropped from his mouth, but she remained pressed against him. Dominik drew a deep breath, distracted by her nearness. He kept his voice low, as she had. "There is no Herr Kleingard, is there? He is you."

A faint smile graced her lips. "Well done, 'Brezelgeist.'" His code name, 'Pretzel Ghost,' sounded silly when she said it, like she couldn't decide whether to laugh or roll her eyes. "Including you, now three people know that secret. It used to be four."

Dominik eyed his knife. What had happened to the fourth? "Your cover is so solid," he continued, "that even Herr Abrabanel doesn't know that 'Herr Kleingard' is a woman. If he'd known, he would have warned me."

She nodded, indicating for him to continue. She hadn't killed him yet, so he did.

"Your brazen behavior in the kitchen was an act? Yes. It was part of your cover. A layer of falsehood to make everyone underestimate you."

Hildegard's eyes twinkled, and she pressed herself even closer. "Rule number three: A pretty face can hide a devious mind. And you," her eyes flashed that sultry look again, "are quite pretty." She was trying to distract him.

Heaven help him if it wasn't working. Dominik tried to focus. "But you agreed to train me. There is no way for that to happen and maintain your cover...unless I agree to keep your secret."

"Or if you never survive your interview." The bared blade waggled.

"You're not going to kill me," he said.

Her eyebrow arched. "You think women can't kill?"

"I think that explaining the body of a man you just met wouldn't be easy. No," he shook his head, "this is all a test, a chance to determine what kind of man I am." Dominik slowly wrapped his fingers over Hildegard's and retrieved his knife. She let him, and he slipped it back into his belt without taking his eyes off hers. "So, did I pass?"

Her expression revealed nothing. "That depends. Can you study under a woman? Can you follow my commands and training without complaint? There's a reason I've never taken an apprentice. Most men are too proud to take orders from a woman."

Dominik placed his hands on Hildegard's shoulders and gently pushed her back. After their near-intimate closeness, the air between them felt cold. "I'm not like most men," he said firmly. "I will follow where you lead. I will be your apprentice."

"Good," she said. Her broad smile was like sunshine after rain. Her hand—the one that had initially been over his mouth—slipped a second knife into a hidden pocket in the front of her dirndl. It was small, a paring knife whose handle and blade were no longer than Dominik's palm.

A sharp knife didn't have to be big to be deadly.

A chill crawled down Dominik's spine like a spider. Had she really been prepared to kill him? He drew a calming breath. He'd volunteered for the clandestine life, happy to serve Herr Abrabanel and the up-timers in Grantville, but he hadn't realized until that moment just how high the stakes truly were. Spies who got caught didn't live long.

If Hildegard noticed his chilling epiphany, she didn't show it. Instead, she turned to peer through the bushes. Satisfied that the coast was clear, she beckoned him back into the courtyard. "For your first assignment," she said, "you're going to meet the master of the Residenz."

"The Elector of Saxony?" Dominik frowned as he followed. Nobody had seen them. Only the woodsman and his son remained in the courtyard, just finishing their unloading with the heavy *thump* of split wood being stacked against the wall. Their attention was firmly on their work.

"Please," Hildegard said without turning, her verbal eyeroll clear. "You think John George would run his own house? The elector is too busy drinking and hunting—usually at the same time. No, we're going to meet someone much more powerful: Herr Deiner, the Hofmeister. Your assignment is to convince him to hire you."

* * *

Herr Deiner was the dour-faced noble Dominik had seen in the courtyard. Hildegard briefed him on the basics as they walked. He asked about the other noble they'd seen, the short, plump man with the gold braiding.

Hildegard grunted as they climbed a short flight of stone steps. "That was Benedict Carpzov, the elector's most trusted advisor. He's a lawyer and a sadistic piece of work if you weren't born with a silver spoon in your mouth. Avoid him at all costs."

Dominik nodded. "Duly noted."

They soon reached Herr Deiner's office and entered after Hildegard's perfunctory knock elicited a sharp, "Come!" The Hofmeister sat behind an excruciatingly neat desk. His personality matched his severe expression. This was clearly a man whose only joys in life came from accounting ledgers and perfectly ironed creases.

The Hofmeister did, in fact, have an opening for which he thought Dominik was eminently qualified. The stables always needed help mucking out stalls. It was a demotion from his previous job as a coachman, the job he had tried to get hired for, but Dominik didn't complain. At least he got to be around horses again.

* * *

For two months, he did little more than establish himself as the newest member of the Residenz staff. He was given a closet of a room in the servants' quarters, only two doors down from Hildegard's room. The unsegregated quarters were a hodgepodge of families, bachelors, and widows living in whichever room was available when they moved in. Hildegard was a widow whose two grown sons now lived out in Dresden proper.

During the hot summer days, Dominik worked in the stables. The evenings he spent in Hildegard's room.

"Why do we have to meet here?" he asked after she closed the door behind them. "The palace grounds are expansive, so surely there's somewhere more discreet where we could train. Everyone thinks that I'm your lover!"

"And you think arranging secret rendezvouses under moonlight would squash those rumors? At least here I can guarantee nobody is listening in," Hildegard said, kicking off her shoes by the door. As usual, she dropped her 'woman on the hunt' act the second they were alone. She was like a changeling, adopting the right face for every occasion. However, she never actually stopped flirting with him. It was enough to make Dominik wonder: did she like him as much as she pretended?

Something about the idea of a moonlit rendezvous brought a wistful smile to Hildegard's face as she dropped onto the bed to tug off her stockings. Was it memories of her dead husband making her smile? Or was she contemplating such a rendezvous with Dominik? The gentle lift of her lips made her even more beautiful. Not like a flower, flowers were too fleeting, but like an oak in springtime: solid, dependable, and full of life.

It was rare that he caught a look at the true Hildegard, the woman beneath her façades. She was a fifth-generation Dresdener who'd married a young baker and given birth to four children. Two hadn't survived childhood, but her two remaining sons were alive and well, running their own bakery out in the city. Her husband was the one who'd brought Hildegard into the clandestine life. He was a secret Jew and a paid informant for the Abrabanel family. After he died twelve years ago, she continued his work.

And she thrived at it.

Dominik realized he was staring. He looked away. He kept his eyes averted as she pulled up her skirts to remove her long stockings. The room was cozy, with a bed, a trunk, a washstand, and a small wardrobe.

"It's the principle of the matter," he continued. "I'm a good Christian man. I haven't been with another woman since Greta died, and the idea that everyone thinks we're living in sin—"

"That's the entire point!" Hildegard said. "If people think they know what's going on, they'll never dig deeper. Rule number thirty-two: The best cover stories are simple and believable."

"I thought that was rule twenty-seven?"

"No, that's, 'The only luck you can count on is bad luck.'"

"Right." Dominik made a mental note. It would have been easier if he could write these rules down, but that would run him afoul of rule number seven: Anything written down *will* be intercepted.

There was a grunt, and Hildegard said, "Ah, that's better." Dominik turned back to see her wiggling her freed toes on the worn throw rug. She pushed herself upright and stepped close, her green eyes boring deep into

Dominik's. "If you're worried about what people think, then you're in the wrong profession. In this job, you will lie, steal, cheat, and maybe even kill. You might even have to," she gave an exaggerated gasp and covered her mouth in faux shock, "kiss a woman you aren't married to."

Dominik raised his hands in defeat, ignoring the way his pulse quickened at the thought. Despite his protests, he enjoyed Hildegard's company. A lot. "Okay, point made."

Hildegard's nod said that his acquiescence was a foregone conclusion. It usually was. "Good. Now, I think it's time to put your training to the test. Remember rule number twelve?"

"Servants are invisible to everyone except other servants?"

"Yes. However, most servants will still ignore you so long as you have a pretext for being wherever you are."

"Something simple and believable."

"Exactly. This palace is full of secrets, many of which I already know—"

"Because you are as devious as you are beautiful," Dominik said before his mind caught up with his words. His jaws snapped shut.

Hildegard arched back and eyed him with delighted shock. "Look at you, learning how to charm the ladies. Keep it up, and I might have to kiss you."

"I...uh..." Dominik stammered. Despite two months around Hildegard, she could still throw him off his stride.

"Your mission is to learn a secret," she continued as though nothing had happened. "You will surveil one of the elector's five children in residence. I don't care which one, take your pick."

Dominik cleared his throat. "*Any* secret? That seems rather broad."

Hildegard patted Dominik's bearded cheek. "I'm sure you can handle it, my little Brezelgeist."

"And if I get caught?"

"Rule number thirty-three: Never admit your true duties. Stick to your story like your life depends on it. It does."

She sat on the bed again, and Dominik leaned against the wardrobe. They discussed the fine art of spycraft late into the night. His mind remained focused on the discussion, but his gaze kept drifting to her lips. Their relationship was clearly defined: master and apprentice. Despite her endless flirting, that's all they were to each other.

And yet.

Dominik wondered what it would be like to kiss her.

* * *

To properly surveil the teenage nobility, Dominik needed easier access throughout the palace than a stableman had. So he began to cheerfully offer a helping hand to other servants whenever and wherever he could. Word quickly spread. Within a month, he was known as the go-to person whenever someone had a duty they needed help with or didn't want. It resulted in a lot of dirty jobs and heavy lifting, but he soon became a recognized face in every corner of the palace.

Recognized, at least, by the servants. He doubted the nobility even knew he existed...which was exactly how he wanted it.

Of the five children in residence, Dominik initially targeted John George II, the nineteen-year-old heir. All he learned, however, was that the heir preferred music and art over politics and intrigue. His only secret was an open one. He suffered from insomnia and had a penchant for sneaking into the conservatory late at night. He would play the viola badly for an hour before returning to bed, soothed by the instrument's cat-screeching torture.

The elector's only daughter in residence was Magdalene Sibylle. She shared her eldest brother's love of music and seemed to devote her life to reading, prayer, and silent contemplation. From a spy's perspective, she was downright boring. Dominik quickly moved on.

Moritz, the youngest at twelve, seemed to have no secrets at all. He was a chatterbox who bent the ear of anyone who would listen, Dominik included. For a while, Dominik thought that perhaps Moritz might let some secret of his siblings slip, but though the boy never stopped talking, he also never said much of consequence.

That left Augustus, who was seventeen, and Christian, who was sixteen. Both had the arrogant swagger of teenage nobility, but it was Christian who seemed the most...squirrelly, for lack of a better term. While Augustus was drab, dull, and blunt to a fault, Christian seemed constantly on edge. It was like he lived his life in an eternal state of trying, and failing, to prove himself.

Dominik finally got his break during a thunderstorm in mid-August. The weather had been hot and miserable for weeks, so the rain was a welcome reprieve. As the skies emptied themselves like the Deluge, Dominik and a dozen other servants wandered the halls. Not at random, but at Herr Deiner's behest. The overly fussy Hofmeister insisted they check the window caulking for leaks. He wanted the castle to be watertight by winter. Dominik volunteered to inspect the wing with the royal apartments.

Extravagant opulence surrounded him as soon as he left the servants' halls. Gilded mirrors reflected painted ceilings, scrollwork sconces, and the occasional flash of lightning from the high windows. His footsteps were perfectly silent on the plush carpet, a stark contrast to the servants' quarters.

He ghosted along the hallway. Der Brezelgeist was on the hunt. He glanced at the windows, making mental notes of two very minor leaks, but his attention remained fixed on the doors at the corner of the hall. Christian's room.

He stopped before the tall double doors and raised his hand to knock. If the princeling was out, Dominik could search his room for some secret to pass on to Hildegard. If he were in, Dominik would perform his window inspection unobtrusively, observing Christian as the prince ignored him.

Voices murmured from behind the door. Dominik's hand froze. He cocked his head. Two voices, male and female. Their words were muffled, but they sounded young. The young man—Christian, he assumed—sounded pleased and petulant at the same time. He was demanding something. The young woman was submissive, but with the sultry tone Dominik had come to recognize from his time around Hildegard.

They were approaching the door.

Dominik's shoulders tensed. He looked around. There was nowhere to hide. He scrambled down the hall and leaned over the windowsill, tracing caulk as if his life depended on it.

It just might.

The door opened, and from the corner of his eye, Dominik saw a young chambermaid slip into the hall. She turned, straightening her dirndl, and froze when she saw Dominik.

He pretended not to see her, his focus resolutely on examining the window. He even grumbled something about shoddy craftsmanship and wiped a damp finger on his trousers. The girl remained frozen like a deer, so Dominik straightened and moved to the next window down the hall. This one's leak was worse than he'd initially noted, a constant stream as the rain hammered against the glass. Lightning crackled outside, followed closely by a crash of thunder that rattled the windows.

When he spared a glance back down the hall, the girl had slipped away, disappearing silently down the other hallway while his back was turned. Dominik grinned. He hadn't gotten a good look at her beyond young and blonde, but that didn't matter. He'd achieved his mission. He'd discovered a secret, and it was a big one.

The elector's son was bedding a servant. For most nobility, that would be as noteworthy as saying they ate breakfast. However, John George was generally a pious man. Dominik doubted he would look kindly on his son's indiscretions.

With a spring in his step, Dominik headed for the kitchen to tell Hildegard.

* * *

It was a long trek around the Residenz Schloss from the apartments to the kitchen, but Dominik had no desire to cut across the rain-soaked inner courtyard. Despite a strong urge to run, he forced himself to walk sedately as though focused solely on his window inspections. People notice haste. A servant simply doing his job is invisible.

The thought of seeing Hildegard brought a ghost of a smile to Dominik's lips. Yes, he saw her most days, but her vibrant presence warmed him in a way he hadn't known for far too many years. Perhaps it was time to admit his feelings to himself.

Yes, it was past time. He was in love, well and truly. It had been twenty years since Greta died, and he wasn't getting any younger. But spies weren't supposed to love. That was rule number nine. Connections were liabilities.

What should he do?

Finally, Dominik rounded the last corner and pushed into the kitchen. The clatter of pans and the smell of hot stew washed over him. Johanna—the young cook who'd admired Dominik's roguish good looks when he'd first arrived—was chopping vegetables into a large pot. A startled look crossed her face. It disappeared so fast he might have imagined it, replaced by a warm smile.

"Dominik, I wondered when you'd drop in! Here to steal *Brezeln* or just my heart?"

Dominik plucked a hot pretzel from its pan. "Find yourself a younger man, Johanna. My heart knows only one love." He gazed longingly at the pretzel, kissed it tenderly, then took a bite. He groaned with exaggerated pleasure. The only way to survive the kitchen staff's ribald ribbing, he'd learned, was to give as good as he got. Besides, they didn't mean anything by it. They all knew he was supposedly Hildegard's man.

Perhaps it was time to make it official.

He took another bite, genuinely savoring the fresh, soft, chewy bread topped by rough salt. He glanced around. "Where's Hildegard?"

Johanna's gaze flicked to the storage room before snapping back to Dominik's. "She's busy. Why don't you come back in half an hour?"

"I won't take two minutes of her time." He turned toward the storage room.

Johanna scrambled from behind the stewpot and stopped him with a hand on his arm. "She's, uh, in a mood. For your own good, have another pretzel and come back later."

"I'm sure I can lighten her mood." He waggled his eyebrows suggestively. He was finally getting comfortable with his cover as Hildegard's lover. Perhaps that was because he wanted it to be true. Besides, he was sure his secret about Christian's dalliance with the maid would lighten her mood immensely. She loved being the bearer of secrets.

Johanna tugged at his arm. "Don't—"

The storage room door opened, and Dominik's heart stilled. A man stepped out. He was younger than Dominik with the powerful build of someone used to heavy labor. His clothes named him a workman, and his satisfied smirk named him a prick. He pushed back rain-slicked hair and swung a dripping cloak around his shoulders. With a wink at Johanna, he strode to the courtyard door like he owned the place. The man completely ignored Dominik. He flipped his hood over his head and pushed through the door, disappearing into the rain.

Resounding thunder was the only sound Dominik heard. Silence didn't exactly fall, but it felt like it. The voices and clattering cookware faded into the background. All he heard was the pounding of the rain outside and the thudding of his own heart.

Johanna's hand fell away from his arm. His gaze flicked back to the storage room. Hildegard stepped out, patting her hair to ensure her crown plait was still in place. Her cheeks were flushed. She froze when she saw Dominik, but only for a moment. She knew what he'd just seen. Yet, like the changeling she was, she threw on a broad smile and sashayed over.

"Hello, handsome. Stop in to warm up? Nasty weather today."

She acted as though nothing had happened. As if he hadn't just seen...

Dominik struggled to speak around the lump in his throat. The bread felt like lead in his stomach. He knew he should pretend nothing happened. The whole point of coming here to train in spycraft was to learn the arts of deception. He had to hide his feelings, smile broadly, and do what needed to be done.

He couldn't do it. His heart wouldn't let him. The best he managed was to turn back to a stricken-looking Johanna. He said, "Thank you for the pretzel," and stormed out of the kitchen.

* * *

Hildegard found him in his room an hour later. She didn't bother knocking; she just barged right in, closed the door much more gently than it deserved—Dominik had slammed it when he returned—and leaned back against the aged wood. He sat on his low cot, leaning against the cold stone wall.

Silence stretched between them. Hildegard crossed her arms beneath her breasts and stared as though demanding that he speak first. Finally, he did.

"It's all a game to you, isn't it?"

"The most exciting game in the world." She nodded. "You've never known a thrill like holding a piece of knowledge that you know nobody else has."

Dominik grunted. "Actually, I do. I found the secret you sent me after."

"Really?" Hildegard straightened. "What did you learn?"

Dominik ignored the question. "So, in this game you play, what am I? Just another pawn?"

"You're my apprentice. The *only* apprentice I've ever taken on, I might add, despite over two decades of serving the Abrabanel family as their eyes and ears in Dresden. You are here to learn the trade because Herr Abrabanel requested—no, *demanded* that I teach you."

That brought Dominik up short. He'd thought she wanted him here. "I didn't realize I was such a burden. So, where does that leave us?" After all these months, he could have sworn the attraction had been mutual.

"There is no us, remember? Rule number nine: connections are a liability."

Dominik's jaw clenched. She felt nothing for him. "So, you're just toying with me? Like you toyed with that man in the kitchen and every other man you meet?" He felt his voice rising.

"That man," she pointed toward the kitchen, her rising tone matching his, "was just another informant. He slipped through the gates because I have a standing bribe with the guards to let my 'lovers' through. Nobody but you batted an eye at him because *that's* the kind of behavior everyone expects of me."

"You certainly seem to enjoy your role."

"You think I like the dirty looks and the whispered insults? Sure, some people don't care; I feed the gossip mill, but do you know what it's like to be called a whore to your face? To have to smile when you want to slap some sanctimonious maid into the next century?"

"Then why do you do it?" Dominik demanded, thrusting himself off the bed.

"For the thrill of the game! People bring me bits and tidbits, pieces of information to pass along to 'Herr Kleingard,' and I pay them for their trouble. Just like the workman you saw today."

"Yeah. He certainly looked like he got 'payment,'" Dominik sneered.

Hildegard's slap caught him completely off guard. She had a strong arm, and he stumbled back. His calves hit the edge of the bed, and he dropped onto it.

"Of all the people," she said, voice shaking with anger, "I'd have thought you would understand. This is the life we chose. I let you in, told you the truth of who I am. Only my *sons* know that truth! And yet you judge me." At this point, she was looming over Dominik. "*That man* looked like a cat with cream because I paid him three months' salary for the message he just brought. He works at a tavern in town, The Black Lion, and he overheard a secret that demanded a high price, but it was worth it."

"What—" Dominik rubbed his jaw. That had been a helluva slap. "What did you learn?"

By Hildegard's expression, she almost didn't tell him. But she drew a deep breath and said, "There's an assassination plot currently underway to kill Benedict Carpzov."

Dominik blinked stupidly for a moment before his mind caught up with the name. "The elector's advisor? That lawyer in the gold braiding who you don't like?"

"That lawyer," Hildegard snapped, "is responsible for the torture and burning of entirely too many women merely suspected of witchcraft. Or heresy. In his words, "Torture is necessary to find the truth, even if innocents suffer." If he had his way, all of Grantville would burn for the glory of God."

"Okay," Dominik said, "so let him get assassinated. Wouldn't that make the world a better place?"

"It would," Hildegard said, deflating a little, "except for one problem."

"What's that?"

"The plot is designed to make it look like Mike Stearns and the New United States ordered the assassination."

* * *

Before the storm had even cleared, Hildegard sent one of her sons to Grantville to inform Herr Abrabanel of what they'd learned. Hopefully, they'd receive guidance in return before the plot matured. With the state of the roads, however, Dominik doubted he'd return in less than five days.

Dominik felt more alone than he had in years. He sank himself into his work, no longer just surveilling the nobility, but watching everyone as he worked throughout the palace. Hildegard had no information on the assassin. They could be noble or common. The only thing they did know was that the assassination would happen within a week.

Despite the time crunch, Dominik had a hard time focusing. He'd misread the situation with Hildegard badly. She didn't love him. Worse, he'd accused her of actually being the loose woman she pretended to be. He'd betrayed her trust. Half of him wished that he could apologize and return everything to the way it was. The other half knew that mere words wouldn't bridge the divide he'd opened between them.

Hildegard's son returned after three days. He must have nearly killed that horse, but he brought instructions from Herr Abrabanel. Find the traitor and anonymously pass the information to the elector, courtesy of Mike Stearns. That would keep Hildegard's position secure while, hopefully, pushing the elector to support Gustavus Adolphus and the newly formed New United States, rather than opposing them. Hildegard thought an unsigned note on his desk would do the trick.

First, they needed proof. Dominik had to find the traitor.

After three days of fruitless surveillance, Dominik was back in the royal apartments, ostensibly retrieving breakfast dishes for the kitchen while eyeing every guard he passed. Hildegard's handsome informant had come again, this time with better details. The assassin was going to be one of the palace guards, someone who would receive final payment today. Whoever was setting this up—could be anyone, Grantville's enemies were numerous—they had had another meeting in the back room of The Black Lion. They'd been discreet, but not discreet enough.

When Dominik had suggested sending the palace guards to The Black Lion, Hildegard had flatly refused. She'd gained a lot of intelligence from that particular tavern and wouldn't risk her informant being discovered when the questions began.

Dominik strode through opulent hallways with a heavy tray stacked with dishes. The elector and his sons had left early on a hunt, and the privy council was supposed to meet upon his return that afternoon. Dominik's mind spun. Which guard was the assassin? He'd passed several already, some with cheerful greetings, others with barely a nod. He recognized them all. None looked suspicious.

Despite the urgency of his mission, Dominik's thoughts kept returning to Hildegard's blunt assessment of their relationship. Her words ate at him like a cancer.

There is no us. He was her apprentice, nothing more.

Pain, deep and heartfelt, sliced through him like an inquisitor's knife. He'd let himself love for the first time in decades, and this was what he got for his troubles. The ache was almost worse than when Greta died. She'd loved him to the end. Hildegard had never loved him at all.

Dominik rounded a corner near the privy council chambers, lost in his thoughts. He only casually glanced at the two halberd-bearing guards outside the ornate double doors. One was Theodore, a quiet young man who tended to fade into the background, and the other was an older man Dominik didn't recognize. That focused his gaze. The older man was passing something to Theo, a broad-bladed knife contained in a gaudy leather sheath painted brilliant red, white, and blue.

Dominik's breath caught. This was it. These were the assassins.

He stumbled, making his tray rattle. Theo's gaze snapped to him. The young man froze. The older guard looked over, cursed quietly, and pressed the knife into Theo's hand. Then he turned and walked nonchalantly toward Dominik. He didn't lower the halberd or do anything threatening, but Dominik knew that if he let that man reach him, he was dead.

"Hey, Theo," Dominik said loudly as his mind scrambled for a plan, "how's it going?" He continued down the hall as though he hadn't seen anything.

"Uh..." The young man seemed flustered by Dominik's sudden appearance.

"You save up enough money to ask that maid to marry you yet? What was her name? Maria?" Dominik asked. It was a struggle to keep his voice calm. The other guard glanced away as he neared, as though he was ignoring Dominik.

"Anna," Theo said, his gaze fixed on the floor as he tried to hide the red-white-and-blue knife behind him. "I—I got the money." Guilt wove through his words, and for a moment, Dominik felt bad for him. This kid was a disposable pawn to whoever was behind the assassination. They'd paid him his 30 pieces of silver and didn't care if he survived the attempt. In fact, Dominik suspected the approaching guard was supposed to kill Theo once the deed was done.

Speaking of whom, the man had reached Dominik. He gripped his halberd tightly and clenched his jaw.

Dominik struck first. Holding his tray firmly by the handles, he flung its contents at the guard. Crockery and cutlery flew. It clattered and crashed, spilling leftover eggs and sausage and a half-full pitcher of milk across the plush carpet. The man jumped back reflexively, and Dominik yelled at the top of his lungs.

"Help! Assassin!"

As far as plans go, it wasn't great. He was supposed to be a spy, working in the shadows, but he didn't want to get skewered. His only hope was to attract lots of attention and then talk his way free. Words were his best weapon.

The guard swung his halberd at Dominik. He blocked with the metal tray, which buckled at the impact. The *clang* reverberated through the hallway.

"Help! Help!" he yelled, backing away as he blocked two more strikes.

"What is the meaning of this?" a voice thundered from down the hall. Dominik glanced up and saw Benedict Carpzov behind Theo, standing in the doorway to the council chamber.

Theo glanced back at the lawyer. His hand tightened around the knife's gaudy sheath.

The older guard—the fake guard—swung his halberd low and caught Dominik on the ankles. His boots protected him from the blade, but the blow dropped him to one knee.

"Hold!" Carpzov bellowed with such command that the fake guard's blade stopped short of slicing through Dominik's throat. The lawyer pushed past Theo and stormed into the hallway. "I want answers before he dies."

Dominik's attacker looked back over his shoulder. The look he gave Theo could have meant "help me out here" or "stab that noble idiot in the back".

Theo looked conflicted. He stepped up behind Carpzov and said, "Um, my lord. It seems we've caught an assassin." He held up the American knife as evidence.

Carpzov took the sheathed blade. Dominik's heart sank. The lawyer examined the garish sheath before his cold eyes swiveled to Dominik. After a long, hard stare, he spun back to the council chamber.

"Bring him inside. I have questions."

* * *

Calm down, Dominik chided himself as Theo and the other man shoved him into the council chamber. They'd taken his utility knife. He was positive that he wasn't going to walk out of this room under his own power. *Breathe. Remember rule thirty-three: Stick to your story like your life depends on it.*

The chamber was small but ornate. Gilded scrollwork lined everything, and the ceiling was painted with a scene from Greek mythology. Dominik didn't know what legend it was and didn't care. He was too busy figuring out how to avoid dying. An oblong table surrounded by a dozen chairs filled the room. The table's nearest end was stacked with papers and a pen, as though Carpzov had been writing while he waited for the elector to return from his hunt.

"Who are you?" the lawyer said as he took a seat at the end of the table. He half-turned the chair from the table, so he was facing Dominik and the guards.

Dominik grunted when the fake guard shoved him to his knees. Two halberds came to rest on his shoulders. He inclined his head meekly. "My name is Dominik Wagner. I'm just a servant. I was delivering dishes to the kitchen when,"—he hooked a thumb over his shoulder—"he attacked me."

"That's a lie, my lord," the guard growled. "He was coming to kill you."

"Yes..." Carpzov held up the sheathed knife, examining it. "So you said." Over his shoulder, he called, "Bring me wine, and be quick about it!"

Dominik hadn't noticed the servant quietly standing in the corner. Hanz was a member of the elector's personal staff, a man with a permanent twitch from dealing with the elector's bombastic and often caustic personality. Dominik and Hanz were on friendly terms. He'd helped the man move some beer barrels for the elector just last week. Hanz's wide eyes flicked from Dominik to Carpzov.

"My lord, I don't have any wine. Only beer for the elector when he returns from the hunt." John George drank a *lot* of beer. Hanz stuttered, "B—but there is wine in the cellar."

"Then go to the cellar!" Carpzov roared.

Hanz jumped before he sketched a shallow bow and fled from the room through a small servant's door at the far end.

Once the door closed, Carpzov unsheathed the American knife. He examined its edge. "Now, let's start again, *Dominik*." He said the name like a curse. "Who do you work for, and why are you trying to assassinate me?"

Dominik gulped.

"Who do you work for, assassin?" Carpzov spat.

Stick to your story. "My lord," Dominik said with all the diffidence he could muster, "I'm just a member of the household staff. I do odd jobs around the palace, and I was helping the kitchen retrieve the breakfast trays."

Carpzov's punch caught Dominik by surprise, striking his jaw like a brick with the knife's hilt. One second, he was on his knees, and the next, he was on the floor, blinking through blinding pain.

The lawyer leaned forward, elbows on his knees. "Who *are* you? Are you a spy?" He growled the question. "I've known for years that there was a spy in the palace."

Dominik's rapidly beating heart went into overdrive. They knew about Hildegard. They knew about her cover. They knew—

No, they didn't know. If the elector or any of his nobles knew that Hildegard was Herr Kleingard, she'd have been executed within a day.

"Tell me," Carpzov continued, "have I finally caught the notorious Herr Kleingard?"

Okay, perhaps he did know something.

Dominik braced one hand on his knee and pushed himself up to a half-kneel, keeping his gaze lowered. The halberds pressed against his shoulders kept him from rising any further. Sticking to his story to the pain of death wasn't going to work. Death would arrive too soon. He had to stop Theo and the other guard from killing both him and Carpzov. He had to escape and warn Hildegard. To do that, he had to break rule thirty-three.

It was time to tell the truth.

"My lord, I work for Herr Kleingard, and we have uncovered an assassination plot to kill you and place the blame at the feet of the Americans." He nodded toward the knife.

Surprise blossomed across Carpzov's face. He glanced at the guards, then back at Dominik. "From what I've heard of these Americans," the lawyer said, "they're all heathens and apostates whose 'technology' sounds suspiciously like witchcraft."

Dominik decided not to argue the point. "My employer is your ally, not your enemy, someone who understands the political ramifications should this plot become known. However, due to the sensitive nature of what I'm about to share, I recommend fewer ears to overhear." He gave a pointed glance over his shoulder at the two guards.

Why hadn't they just killed Carpzov and Dominik both at this point? What were they waiting for?

Carpzov said nothing for a long moment. His gaze flicked from the knife to the guards to Dominik. "No, I think not," he finally said. "I prefer having you under guard."

Guards who want to kill you! Dominik thought, though he wasn't entirely sure about Theo at this point. "There is a traitor in the palace, my lord, a young man who sold his loyalty for, of all things, love." Dominik felt Theo's halberd twitch. "I don't think he's an evil man, merely misguided. It's the man who hired him, however, that you must be wary of." All true or close enough to the truth, so far as Dominik was concerned.

"Oh? How interesting." Carpzov's gaze shifted from the broad-bladed knife to its sheath. Dominik hadn't noticed earlier, but the words "American Patriot" were emblazoned across the leather in bold letters. "Have you any proof?"

Dominik spread his hands, surprised at how easily the lie came to his lips. "The messages I intercepted were damaged in the storm last week when—" He raised a hand. "It's a long story, but I no longer have the evidence I need. That's why I didn't come to you sooner, my lord."

"Interesting," Carpzov said again, as though savoring the word. Despite the danger, Dominik felt a spike of excitement. His lies were getting through to the man. So, this was what Hildegard had meant about the thrill of the game.

And that's when his half-cocked plan fell apart. As if he'd summoned her with his thoughts, Hildegard pushed through the main door holding a tray with a bottle of red wine and a long-stemmed cut-crystal glass. She was a vision of swaying skirts in her low-cut dirndl. She barely even glanced at Dominik kneeling on the floor. She just clucked her tongue, closed the door, and stepped around him to set the wine on the table at Carpzov's elbow.

"Apologies for the delay, my lord," she said. "That klutzy Hanz dropped the first bottle, spilled wine all over himself, and he had to go change his uniform. Such a terrible mess! But here I am, and here," she bobbed a curtsy, managing to sound airheaded and competent at the same time, "is your wine."

Once she'd poured the wine, Hildegard moved to stand unobtrusively against the wall behind Carpzov's chair, silent as a piece of furniture. Her bearing turned servile, eyes downcast, and back stiff in the universal "invisible servant" posture. Dominik had to pry his eyes off her as she settled into position. What was she doing here? She was going to get herself killed!

So were Dominik and Carpzov if he didn't figure out some way out of this. Dominik was pretty sure the only reason he wasn't dead already was because Carpzov was holding the murder weapon.

The guards shifted uneasily as the lawyer took a long, slow drink from his wine. They were getting anxious. This assassination was completely out of control. Dominik's pulse quickened. A halberd behind him twitched.

"Screw this!" the older guard said. "Kill 'em all!" His halberd lifted from Dominik's right shoulder and thrust toward Carpzov. Dominik threw himself to the side as the lawyer twisted in his chair with a surprised yelp. The American knife and his wine glass fell to the floor with a clatter and a shatter. The halberd's long blade pierced the back of the chair with a *thunk* where Carpzov's head had been.

Dominik kicked back, hitting the guard's knee with a satisfying *crack*. The man screamed and fell over the shaft of his halberd, which was still stuck in the chair. He tumbled onto Dominik. His elbow hit Dominik's ribs hard enough to steal his breath. The guard twisted toward him, pulling Dominik's own utility knife from his belt. Murder glittered in his eyes. He raised the blade.

That glitter of death shifted into surprise when Dominik whipped the American knife up to press against the man's throat. The blade had landed nearby, and Dominik had snatched it up.

Rule number two: Always have a weapon ready, even if it's not yours.

Suddenly, the assassin arched back, gasping in pain. His eyes widened before he went limp and collapsed atop Dominik. Behind him stood Theo, his halberd wet with blood, his eyes wide.

Dominik scrambled out from beneath the assassin's corpse while Carpzov scrambled out of his chair. Hildegard hadn't moved from her spot against the wall, though she was watching everything, eyes narrow and calculating. It was like she was working through a problem in her mind and didn't care whether Dominik lived or died while she figured it out.

That hit him like a kick in the gut. He was just an apprentice, nothing more. This was another test to see if he was worthy.

"Stop him!" Carpzov yelled to Theo, pointing as Dominik rolled to his knees. Dominik belatedly realized that he still held the American knife. He dropped it with a clatter as Theo's halberd swung over and stopped just below Dominik's throat.

He froze. "I'm not the assassin, my lord," he said, then gestured to the dead man. He made a point of not looking at Theo, the other half of this plot.

"I know you aren't," Carpzov sneered, "I hired these two idiots to make it look like the Americans had attempted to assassinate me. The elector remains indecisive about them, and this would have solidified his decision. You were just in the wrong place at the wrong time, the perfect scapegoat."

Dominik's jaw would have dropped if there wasn't a blade under it.

"However, you admitted to being a spy, which is a much better catch than I expected. So, *spy*, I offer you a choice. Tell me who Herr Kleingard is now, or tell me when the torturers finish with you. You'll tell me either way. It's just a question of how much pain you wish to endure before you die."

Dominik drew a shuddering breath. It had all been a setup, a scheme of high-level politics not even meant to catch him, but he'd walked right into it.

He was going to die. The temptation to actually tell the truth flared briefly inside him, but he pushed it down. Despite everything, he still loved Hildegard. He would protect her secrets with his life.

"I am Herr Kleingard," he said. "I am the spy you've been looking for."

Carpzov's eyes glittered with delight. "Finally." He gestured to Theo. "Kill this—"

Hildegard struck like a snake. One second, she was against the wall, all but forgotten, the next she was behind Carpzov, her hidden paring knife at his throat. A drop of blood welled beneath her sharp blade. The lawyer froze. He had fallen victim to rule number twelve: Servants are invisible. He'd forgotten she was in the room.

Hildegard spoke softly, death in her voice. "I want you to think long and hard before spilling the blood of the man I love."

Carpzov carefully raised a hand and waved Theo down. The young man looked thoroughly conflicted by this point, but lowered his halberd.

Dominik sagged and drew a gasping breath. Then his mind caught up with what she'd just said. "Wait, you love me? What about 'there is no us'?"

Hildegard cocked her head as though just realizing what she'd said. "Of course I love you, you idiot. I was angry. But I can't let you die. That would make it rather hard to spend the rest of my life with you."

A laugh bubbled in Dominik's chest. Of course, she loved him. She'd fallen as hard as he had; she'd just been better at hiding it. "Did—" he pushed down his laughter, "Did you just propose to me while holding a knife to another man's throat?"

"Of course not," she sniffed indignantly. "I would never be so forward."

"Yes, you would," he said, barely holding in the wholly inappropriate laughter. "You know, some women in Grantville think that women should be able to propose to men. It's the wildest thing." He was babbling, and he knew it. But at least it kept him from giggling as the tension flooded out of him. Spies should not giggle.

"Really?" Hildegard arched a disbelieving eyebrow. "I think I need to talk to these women."

Carpzov carefully cleared his throat. His Adam's apple bobbed beneath Hildegard's blade.

"Right," she said. "Sorry about that, my lord. Let's stay focused on the present, shall we?" She looked at Theo. "Theo, I'm guessing you already got your blood money for your part in this ugly mess." She sounded like a disapproving mother. Theo lowered his eyes and nodded. "Fool. I always knew Anna was too good for you. This snake wasn't going to let you live, no matter what he promised. Like Dominik, you were meant to die after you'd served your purpose. At this point, you really only have one option left." She nodded toward the door. "Leave."

Theo looked at his halberd as though contemplating violence, but instead he dropped it and strode away, careful not to attract attention to himself.

"Now," Hildegard said brightly to Carpzov after Theo was gone. "As much as I'd love to slit your throat and make the world a better place, I think it's time for us to part ways." She shoved him into his chair. He had to lean aside to avoid the halberd blade still dangling from it.

"You'll never escape Dresden," Carpzov growled.

"You won't stop us," Dominik said, full of confidence now that he knew he wasn't going to die. "Chase us, and we tell the world about your assassination plot, how you intended to manipulate your lord and master, the Elector of Saxony. Let us go, and this whole sordid affair remains our little secret. Nobody needs to know." He gave a small bow and scooped up his utility knife and the American one, slipping both into their sheaths. "Until next time." Before the lawyer could respond, he and Hildegard slipped out the door, closing it behind them.

Dominik almost started running, but Hildegard caught his arm. She raised a finger to her lips. They waited, listening for Carpzov's next move. Would he call for help now that he didn't have a knife to his throat, or would pride keep his tongue?

A bellow of rage resounded from the room. A second later, a wine bottle crashed against the door.

Hildegard grinned, and Dominik took her hand. That was all the answer they needed.

* * *

Their escape from Dresden wasn't precipitous, but they didn't dawdle. No point in waiting around for Carpzov to change his mind. Dominik worried that Hildegard might have difficulty abandoning her life, but it actually took him longer to pack his knapsack than it took her. She kept an emergency bag packed, just in case.

Apparently, that was rule seventy-one: Always be ready to walk away.

On their way to the kitchens, Hildegard stopped one of the maids in the hall. Dominik was surprised to realize it was the same girl he'd seen coming out of Christian's room. "Anna, tell the Troll, 'The bridge is his.'" Anna's eyes widened, but she nodded and scurried away.

Dominik eyed Hildegard sideways as they continued toward the kitchens. "Who's the Troll?"

"My number two. I just told him to take over the network. I can only do so much from afar."

"Wait, what? You have a number two? You never mentioned him."

"Of course not!" Hildegard took Dominik's hand. "Rule forty-two, remember?"

"That was the one about compartmentalization, right?"

"Right. Safety trumps everything. *That's* why you never met the Troll, why you didn't even know he existed."

"Okay, but what about your sons? Carpzov could still get to you through them."

Hildegard's lips thinned. "We'll warn them on our way out of town, but they won't leave Dresden. Their lives are here. My boys know how to take care of themselves."

A few steps later, Dominik said, "I never told you the secret I learned about the elector's children. Still want to know?"

"Sure."

"Anna is warming Christian's bed."

"I know," Hildegard said. "She's gotten all kinds of information out of the elector's son. He likes bragging to her. She told me she saw you in the hall that night."

Dominik snorted and rolled his eyes. "Of course she did. Why do I even bother?"

Hildegard barked a laugh.

They soon reached the kitchen, and Hildegard informed Johanna that she was in charge now. The young woman paused halfway through twisting pretzels on a pan. "What?" She looked alarmed. "What's going on?"

"It's a long story involving a knife to Benedict Carpzov's throat," Hildegard said. That got everybody's attention. "So, Dominik and I are running away together."

"She finally asked me to marry her! he added, slipping his arm around her waist.

Johanna snorted and waved a flour-coated hand at them. "Good luck. I love her, but that woman's trouble, let me tell you!" Hildegard squawked at the younger woman with good-natured offense.

"Perhaps," Dominik said, giving Hildegard a long, warm look, "but she's just the kind of trouble I need." He leaned down to kiss his newfound love and murmured, "I wouldn't change her for the world."

It started as a tender kiss, his first since Greta had died. The kitchen crew whooped and catcalled as the kiss deepened. Blood sang in his ears. His fingertips tingled as they tangled in her hair. Hildegard wrapped her strong arms around him, pulling him close, and for a moment, Dominik happily lost track of the world around him.

It seemed the spy's life wasn't going to be so lonely after all.

Columns

The Mannington Minute

Jackie Britton Lopatin

Small town and rural life is unsurprisingly different from life in bigger cities. It has a different rhythm to it. Not that the people have different likes or dislikes, but events have to be cognizant of all the other events going on around them and how well they mesh (or don't mesh!) together.

When I first started thinking about publicizing various Mannington events within the greater 1632 Universe, I optimistically thought I could put together some kind of calendar for the coming year.

Hah!

Too many outdoor events here are dependent on good weather or other factors. One year the Greenery Bazaar (a major fundraiser in early December held by the West Augusta Historical Society) was held on the same weekend as another major event in Fairmont, and it affected sales. Too many worthy causes and too few volunteers.

So, people live and learn. I'm not going to try to publicize everything that might be of interest to fans of the Grantville Universe, except to point out that this area has a lot to offer: beautiful scenery, interesting history, and friendly people. If you're thinking of visiting this area, be sure to check in with the Marion County Visitors Bureau for the very latest regional offerings, as well as the City of Mannington and Mannington Main Street's web and social media presence.

I've heard it said that the reason we don't hold a 1632 convention in Mannington very often is because there's not much to do or see around here. After you've toured the Round Barn and the Wilson School museums, and visited the site of the coal mine disaster, what else is there?

Maybe it's time to go a little farther afield.

Between the exits on I-79 for Morgantown and Bridgeport/Clarksburg, there are exits for Granville (Eric's initial inspiration for the Grantville Universe), Prickett's Fort State Park, Downtown Fairmont (the best way to reach Highway 250 North to Mannington), White Hall (where the Fairmont Walmart is located, along with the most likely convention hotels), and an exit to East Grafton.

Grafton? As a tourist attraction of interest to the science fiction/Grantville crowd?

This small town in Taylor County, near the Tygart Lake State Park, has about 5,000 residents, but its historic district is also the home of the Grafton Monster Museum, based on the rumored 1964 sighting of what was dubbed "The Grafton Monster." On June 12 and 13, 2026, Grafton will be hosting the third annual Grafton Monster Street Fair, and I'm planning to attend it. It's about a thirty-minute drive from the Fairmont Walmart, so for me the idea of mixing with other SF fans close to home sounds great. If we can figure out how to boost interest in the 1632 Universe, that sounds even better.

Specialized craft fairs and street markets can be financially rewarding to local small businesses, so West Virginia is interested in promoting anything that may boost tourism, like the annual Mothman Festival in Point Pleasant, WV, based on the 2010 movie.

If you craft a product to sell at street fairs or science fiction conventions, you'll be following in the grand tradition of Mannington's own Russell Fluharty, also known as "The Dulcimer Man." During the summertime he would travel around to different county fairs and street festivals performing folk music and demonstrating the hammer dulcimers he had for sale. Before the winter storms closed him and his wife onto their farm for months at a time, he made sure he had enough materials to make nine dulcimers during this down time to sell during the upcoming playing season. Farming of a different sort.

Fluharty was a driving force behind the creation of the West Augusta Historical Society and its initial purchase of the Wilson School. The book about his life, "The Dulcimer Man," written by his daughter, Twila Dawn Fluharty, is still available through Amazon, and videos of his playing can be viewed on YouTube.

You can never tell in what direction an idea will take you, but if you like it, odds are others will, too.

Historic Gems Restorations

Most of you have probably never visited Mannington, WV, the town Eric Flint modeled Grantville on, but you've almost certainly seen towns like it. You might even be from one. There are some gorgeous old homes and businesses in the downtown area, but not as many as there were in 1999 (when Eric visited Mannington) or even a few years ago. It's a constant drip, drip, drip of loss, one lovely old building at a time succumbing to age, neglect, or plain bad luck. A once-packed downtown is now half vacant lots and half buildings that need a bit of TLC. The historic homes are a mish-mash of restorations, projects, and even a few derelicts.

There was an old apartment building on Water Street in Mannington that was torn down by 2008. The building next to it, at Pleasant and Water, had clearly been stunning once, but by 2003 it had a tree growing out the second story window and by 2004 it was gone. The chiropractor's office at Main and Market is for sale. The fireplaces and woodwork are stunning, but the exterior water damage on the second-floor bay windows is worse every year, and the side yard is getting overgrown.

We visited in October 2022. By our next visit one year later, several homes in the historic district had been razed. But the renovations on a painted lady across from the Catholic Church were completed, and a unique home down Furbee had finished some renovations.

Mannington is like so many small towns across the USA that are long past their heyday. It has some beautiful old buildings. A few are well-maintained or restored and a joy to see. A few are so badly deteriorated there isn't much choice other than to tear them down. But in the middle? That's where help is needed. The buildings that still have "good bones." The ones that are still standing, but may need new windows, or a paint job, or vegetation cut back. They may have damage from the last flood (Mannington floods) or from years of neglect. But they are still standing, and they need some love. That's where Historic Gems Restorations enters the picture for Mannington.

First United Presbyterian Church, Mannington, WV, in 2022

We've all heard the story about someone walking down the beach and throwing starfish back. Someone says it doesn't make a difference, and they reply that it makes a difference "to this one." The 1632 community can help Historic Gems make a difference to this one small town, a place that was dear to Eric Flint and holds a special place in his widow's heart as well. A place we can walk through and see a different world, quite literally.

Historic Gem Restorations is a non-profit dedicated to the preservation of historic buildings in Mannington, West Virginia. They have been awarded grants for exterior facelifts to several buildings in downtown Mannington. These include:

2024

205 Market Street – Sweet P's restaurant.

2025

116 Market Street – Morris Marketplace Menagerie

116 Buffalo Street – The Mystery Vault escape room

115 Market Street – The Show Building. In Mannington, it's the old movie theater. (But not the old, old movie theater, which was across the street.) In Grantville, it's also the movie theater—and functional because when Eric visited in 1999, all the equipment was still in the building, so it came back through the Ring of Fire.

111 Market Street – Mountaineer Florist

If you walk around Mannington with Bjorn Hasseler, or Bethanne Kim, or Mike Knopp, or some of the other writers, they can tell you where to go for the best pizza in Grantville. They can describe which businesses are on an empty lot, and direct you to the grocery stores in Grantville. They can tell you why the Bridal Saloon (wine bar) is located near the train station and how an arsonist tried to burn down the building at Market and Water Streets but was foiled—in the 1632 universe. (In the real universe, the building burnt.) We are undoubtedly biased, but we think that connection makes Mannington special, and we want to help it keep the historic buildings that are still there.

We encourage you to follow the Historic Gem Restorations Facebook page to keep up to date on all they are doing.

https://www.facebook.com/profile.php?id=61555858332917

It's now seeking a grant for further restoration of the movie theater. It also has a Go Fund Me page to replace three windows in the outside ticket area and two windows in the movie poster area:

https://www.gofundme.com/f/donate-to-restore-mannington-theater-windows?attribution_id=sl:e4e8de48-c3b5-4ed5-b583-b3d0c94d0972&lang=en_US&ts=1760479234

As time passes, Mannington and Grantville diverge. If you've joined us on Baen's Bar (baensbar.net) or Facebook (https://www.facebook.com/groups/113392810011) or at a convention, you know that Mannington and Grantville were never exactly the same—just very, very close.

The Ring of Fire took Grantville from 2000 to 1631. The leading edge of plot is in mid-1637 now. It's been just over six years in-story, while twenty-five years have passed in the real world. Grantville's buildings are where Mannington's were about 2006, except that Grantville had a pressing need for first housing and then businesses, so a lot of renovations happened in 1631-1633 that didn't happen in Mannington. We would like to see Mannington thrive, and the survival of the historic district is part of that. Eric Flint's 1632 & Beyond will feature some news and events from Mannington and Marion County, especially if we can pass along opportunities for you to be involved.

1632con

Since 2003, the 1632 universe has gathered every year, in Mannington, within another convention, or online.

Here's where we've been the past few years:

2020	ROFCON	virtual
2021	Capclave	Rockville, Maryland
2022	Mannington	Mannington, West Virginia
2023	Mannington	Mannington, West Virginia
2024	FantaSci	Durham, North Carolina
2025	Fencon	Dallas, Texas

Here's where we'll be next year:

2026	Philcon	Cherry Hill, New Jersey

Philcon is the oldest science fiction convention in the United States, established in 1936. It's been across the Delaware River from Philadelphia, in Cherry Hill, New Jersey, for the past eighteen years. Its website is and should be updated for 2026 soon.

Philcon is normally the weekend before Thanksgiving, and with 2026 being the 250th anniversary of our independence, it's a great time to visit the National Park Service sites. Independence National Park includes Independence Hall, where our Constitution was drafted, as well as the Liberty Bell and the Benjamin Franklin Museum. If you are interested in the Amish, Lancaster isn't far away in Pennsylvania and is home to the oldest and largest Amish community in the US.

Philcon is accessible by car, bus, train, and plane. For our international readers, the last Thursday of November is our Thanksgiving and while most people aren't traveling that day, but travel for the rest of the week is some of the heaviest of the year. We hope you will join us there, and we will supply additional information as it becomes available.

Available Now

Mrs. Flannery's Flowers, Gourmets of
Grantville, Red Shield

Available Now

Mrs. Flannery's Flowers, Gourmets of
Grantville, Red Shield

Mrs. Flannery's Flowers
Bethanne Kim

Big things are happening in Grantville since it was sent through time and space to war-torn seventeenth-century Germany, and up-timer nursing student Krystal Reed isn't handling it very well. She never wanted to live in Grantville and being sent back to the seventeenth century just makes it worse. Working with doctors who think bleeding is a legitimate medical practice and that women have no business in medicine is exasperating, to say the least—but their prejudices are no match for the new medical programs in Grantville and Jena. Now if only she can recover from losing her parents, her friends, her home, her college, and her future.

Nils Jorgensen and family are just a few of the thousands of down-timers looking for a new future in Grantville. They arrive with little more than their skills. Through hard work, the Jorgensens start a fashion empire.

For the elderly Irene Flannery, life is more about smaller, personal issues. With no family left up-time, her biggest worry now that's she's in the seventeenth century is having a married curate at the Catholic church. (The scandal!) But she has kept a secret since FDR was President and she'll defend her rose bushes to the death because of it.

https://www.baen.com/mrs-flannery-s-flowers.html

The Gourmets of Grantville
Bethanne Kim

After traveling through time and space from 2000 in West Virginia to 1631 in Germany, the Grantvillers have to find enough food, medicine, and other supplies to stay alive and healthy while helping their new German neighbors and a constant flow of refugees do the same. Working together, they grow and gather enough food for everyone, but it's not quite what anyone is used to eating. Down-time Germans view potatoes as animal food, unfit for human consumption — until they try their first potato chips. Seeing everyone, including small children, drinking beer instead of water is a big change for the up-timers, just as big a change as seeing people casually drink water and not get sick is for down-timers. But the Grantville Cooking Club proves food is also a bridge, helping up-timers and down-timers work together to create a new cuisine. They also jump-start several new restaurants and businesses.

Meanwhile, regular life continues. How do you keep going when you know that your child, or spouse, will die because life-saving medicine or surgery isn't available in 1631? How do you cope with watching them slowly die from something that was curable, before? Greg Ferrara, Linda Bartolli, and Phillip Bartolli are forced to face these questions when the Ring of Fire happens weeks before Tina was scheduled for lifesaving surgery that, like her life-saving medication, is no longer available.

And what do you do when your wife really wants a bagel with cream cheese but they haven't been invented yet?

https://www.baen.com/gourmets-of-grantville.html

Red Shield
Bethanne Kim

Big battles may be fought with APCs and battleships, but when small West Virginia town goes back through time and space to land in Thuringia, Germany in 1631, there are bigger battles to fight. Ones the military might struggle with. The kind meant for octogenarians, parents, and teens. Whether their goal is preserving the past, ensuring the future, or making the world a better place, these volunteers aren't going to accept "it can't be done" as the answer.

Some of their goals may sound simple — teaching hand washing for Pete's sake! — but the missions of the Red Cross and Scouts have never been more important, and their tools more in need of evolving, to win the hearts and minds of the new world that surrounds them than in the 1630s.

No matter what the tool or the fight, Grantvillers are ready for battle and the world better "Be Prepared" for *Stayin' Alive* West Virginia style!

https://www.baen.com/red-shield.html

Coming Soon

The Marshals, Time Spike: The Mysterious Mesa, Time Spike: The First Cavalry of the Cretaceous, Saving the Dodo

Coming Soon

The Marshals, Time Spike: The Mysterious Mesa, Time Spike: The First Cavalry of the Cretaceous, Saving the Dodo

The Marshals
Mike Watson

The New United States is about to join the United States of Europe, becoming the State of Thuringia and Franconia. The Thirty Years' War is still being waged. Armies cross and re-cross the German states. With war comes lawlessness, and with lawlessness comes the need for law and order.

Who can fill this enforcement niche better than three retired old soldiers, known to down-timers as the *Die Drei Alten Soldaten?* Archie Mitchell, Harley Thomas, Max Huffman, retired US Army Master Sergeants who, with their apprentice, Dieter Issler, use their up-time experience as Deputy Sheriffs, to become the first Marshals of the newly created District Court system of the SoTF.

The Marshals are little known until Thomas Bloem and his sister, Maria D'Angelo, brother and sister journalists, arrive to interview them. They record the formation of the Marshal's Service and the three Marshals, from their first case as Marion County Deputy Sheriffs, until they leave Grantville to provide law and order throughout the State of Thuringia and Franconia.

Coming February 3, 2026

https://www.baen.com/the-marshalls.html

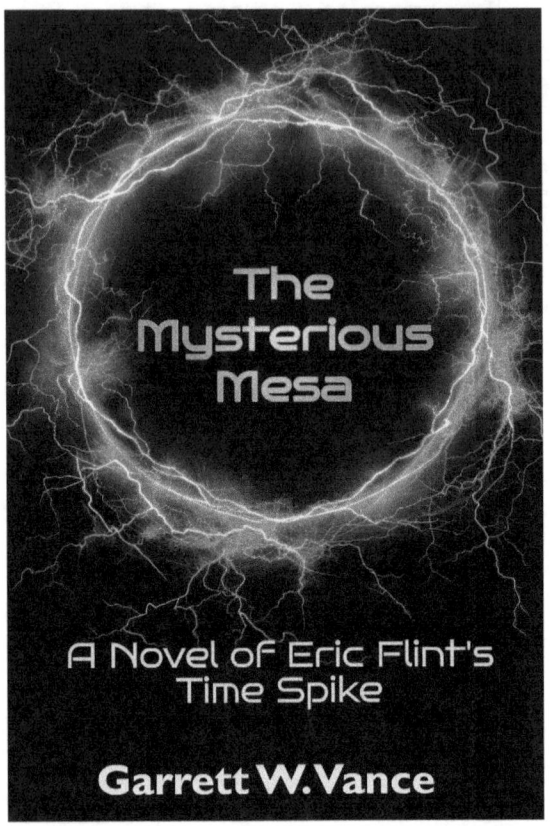

Time Spike: The Mysterious Mesa
Garrett W. Vance

In the world of the second Assiti Shard, four friends from different time periods explore their new world.

Coming February 3, 2026

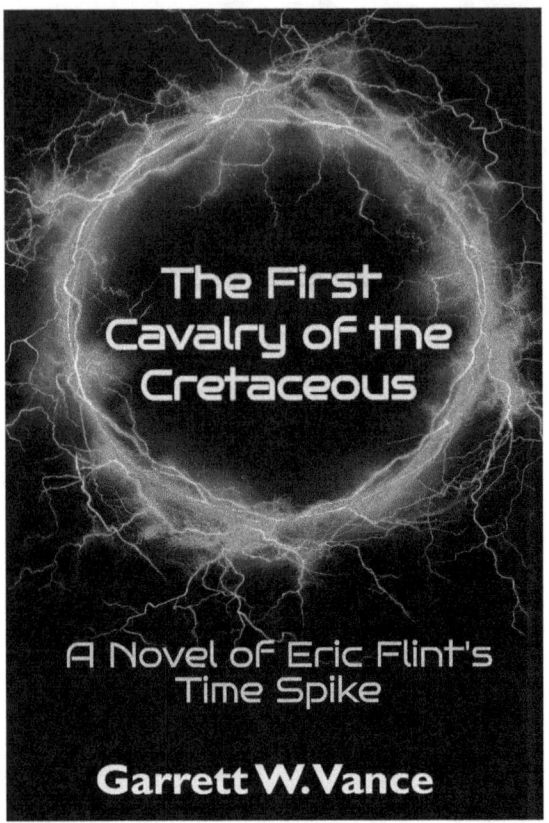

Time Spike: The First Cavalry of the Cretaceous
Garrett W. Vance

When faced with enemies from different time periods, the challenges of a new world, and dinosaurs, what do you need? Cavalry.

Coming March 3, 2026

Saving the Dodo
Garrett W. Vance

In the 1630s, dodos were still alive. Princess Kristina means to keep it that way.

Coming April 7, 2026

Supporting the 1632verse

We appreciate our readers, and we thank you for continuing to support the 1632 universe. None of the things in this section are likely to be news to most of our readers, but here are some ways you can support us more.

Reviews

This is pretty straight-forward: Books that have more reviews (especially positive ones) are promoted more, so we need our readers to review our books.

So pretty please and thank you, take a minute to review this book. And if you leave a comment in addition to stars, know that we will read it and we appreciate the time you take for those comments!

Give a 1632 Gift

1632 is a free download from Baen. Issue 1 of Eric Flint's 1632 & Beyond is a free download on 1632Magazine.com and Baen. Please share them with anyone you think might get hooked!

You can give (or receive) a gift subscription to 1632 & Beyond. Just choose "gift" when you add it to your cart.

 We also have some branded items available to buy on our Zazzle store. There is a coffee mug with the Hangman Regiment logo, an Apple watch band with a becky (currency), and a wine bottle tote with the cover from Issue 2. We hope you find something fun you enjoy! If you have a suggestion for something new, just let us know and there's a good chance we'll add it.

https://www.zazzle.com/store/1632_and_beyond

Buy Another Issue

There are 102 volumes of the Grantville Gazette and a new issue of 1632 & Beyond every other month. That's a lot! Have you read them all? If not, bundles of six (one year of the magazine) are a great way to save some money. They are priced at six for the cost of five.

Buy a 1632 Baen Novel

The Grantville Gazette and now Eric Flint's 1632 & Beyond are the short story venues for the 1632verse and Baen publishes the novels. While we (obviously) benefit more directly from magazine purchases, we still benefit indirectly when you buy novels from Baen. Some of us also benefit directly as authors receiving royalties.

The Baen books fall roughly into two categories right now. First, the mainline novels. These are generally the ones released in hardback and then paperback in addition to ebooks. (Again, roughly speaking.) Then there are the ebook only releases. As of 2026, the majority of these were originally published by Ring of Fire Press, but there are two fully new novels (*Security Solutions* by Bjorn Hasseler and *Red Shield* by Bethanne Kim). Baen has provided new covers and polished all the former RoFP novels a bit more before re-releasing them.

 There are dozens of mainline books from Baen. The link below lists them all by publication date. There are also links to a list chronological within the universe and one by storyline.

https://author.1632magazine.com/canon-continuity/1632-books-by -publication-date/

Connect with us on Social Media

We would love to hear from you here at *Eric Flint's 1632 & Beyond!* There are lots of ways to get in touch with us and we look forward to hearing from you.

Main Sites

 **Email:** 1632Magazine@1632Magazine.com
Shop: 1632Magazine.com

 **Author Site:** Author.1632Magazine.com
For anyone interested in writing in the 1632verse, or fans interested in more background on the series and how we keep track of everything.

Facebook

Our Facebook Group is our primary social media, but we do use the FB Page, YouTube, and Flickr accounts.

 **Facebook Group:** The Grantville Gazette / 1632 & Beyond

We also have a Facebook Page at Facebook.com/t1632andBeyond.

YouTube

 We have quite a lot on our YouTube Channel because we have videos of most of the panels from at least four separate 1632 Minicons, including FenCon in 2025, FantaSci in 2024, and several with Eric and other now-deceased authors on the panels. In addition, we have playlists with videos of Mannington, the town Grantville was based on. We know we have an international readership, so one of the playlists shows real estate listings for typical Mannington homes, to give y'all a more realistic idea of what they really look like.

YouTube: 1632andBeyond

Flickr

 These images are mostly of Mannington, WV, the town Grantville is based on. There are a lot more ranchers, trailers, and other humble, normal homes than this may lead you to expect because, well, it's more fun to share photos

of a freshly remodeled painted lady than a double-wide with a pickup and two ATVs in the yard.

https://www.flickr.com/photos/199556693@N05/albums

Reviews and More

You are welcome to join us on **BaensBar.net**. Most of the chatting about 1632 on the Bar is in the 1632 Tech forum. If you want to read and comment on possible future stories, check out 1632 Slush (stories) and 1632 Slush Comments on BaensBar.net.

Last but far from least, if you are interested in writing in the 1632 universe, that's fabulous! Please visit **Author.1632Magazine.com** (QR code) for more information.

 Circling back to the very first way to help: Reviews really matter, especially for small publishers and indie authors, so please take a few minutes to post a review online or wherever you find books, and don't forget to tell your friends to check us out!

www.ingramcontent.com/pod-product-compliance
Lightning Source LLC
Chambersburg PA
CBHW051435170626
46809CB00006B/2478